PENGUIN BOOKS

WHEN THE WIND BLOWS

Raymond Briggs was born in Wimbledon Park, London, in 1934. His father, Ernest, was a Co-op milkman for over thirty years and was awarded a certificate when he retired. His mother, Ethel, was 'in service' for over twenty years but received no certificate. At the age of ten, Briggs passed 'The Scholarship' and went to the local Grammar School. Here he had daily speech lessons and learned to become middle class. After five years he was awarded 'The School Certificate'. At the age of fifteen he went to the local art school and after two years he was awarded 'The Intermediate Art Certificate'. After two further years studying painting he was awarded 'The National Diploma of Design (in Painting) Certificate'. He was then conscripted into the army where he attained no rank but was awarded a certificate saying 'Excused Boots'. He studied painting for two more years at the Slade School of Fine Art and here he was awarded 'The Diploma of Fine Art (London University) Certificate'. Since leaving the Slade in 1957 and failing as a painter, he has been a freelance illustrator, book designer and writer producing what are known as 'children's' books. For work in this field he has been awarded several certificates. *When the Wind Blows* represented a dramatic new development, as it was his first 'adult' book which he followed with *The Tin Pot Foreign General and the Old Iron Woman*.

When the Wind Blows **received overwhelming attention from the press. Here are a selection of the reviews:**

'We should all force ourselves to read this grimly humorous and horribly honest book'
– *Sunday Telegraph*

'As powerful and chilling as *The War Game*' – *City Limits*

'Terrifying' – *Oxford Mail*

'A horror story' – *Daily Mirror*

'It's brilliant' – *Labour Weekly*

'It is a funny, frightening book' – *New Statesman*

SOME COMMENTS ON THIS BOOK

extremely effective and timely. It was chilling.
ERIC HEFFER M.P.

It's a remarkable piece of work. I'm sure it will get a great deal of attention, and rightly so.
CLAIRE RAYNER

Horribly realistic. Such a war must be deterred.
LORD HOME OF THE HIRSEL

Very original and clever—unnerving though it is!
DAVID STEEL M.P.

Really good.
TONY BENN M.P.

It raises the gravest questions of our time in the most entertaining and cumulatively persuasive way.
LORD ELWYN-JONES

Both highly original and extremely timely. It should have some influence and cause some re-thinking.
MICHAEL O'HALLORAN M.P.

This House welcomes the publication of "When the Wind Blows" by Raymond Briggs as a powerful contribution to the growing opposition to nuclear armament and hopes that it will be widely read.
Motion put down in the House of Commons by Labour M.P. Mr. JOHN GARRETT. HANSARD 15.2.1982 No.57

A very original approach to the subject and one which everyone will understand.
SIR JULIAN RIDSDALE M.P.

It is a perfectly chilling story of the perilous world we inhabit .... and the climax is calculated to stun the stoutest senses. It is superb.
GLASGOW HERALD

This book deserves a very wide audience and should be compulsory reading for young and old alike.
LABOUR HERALD

This blockbuster of a book cannot fail to entertain, astound and distress any adult wise enough to buy it.
CATHOLIC HERALD

Whatever your politics this is the most eloquent anti-Bomb statement you are likely to read.
DAILY MAIL

extraordinary and original
GODFREY SMITH SUNDAY TIMES

A moving book, a horrifying book, a work of great stature
BARRY TOOK

devastating black comedy - a horribly funny and courageous work
THE GUARDIAN

a devastating book – great tenderness, dignity and compassion. It is _that_ story which we should tell to the children, and we should tell it to them young
BEL MOONEY   SANITY

Acute and not patronising, aching with love and bitterness, it is meant to break your heart to some purpose.
W. L. WEBB THE GUARDIAN

RAYMOND BRIGGS

When the Wind Blows

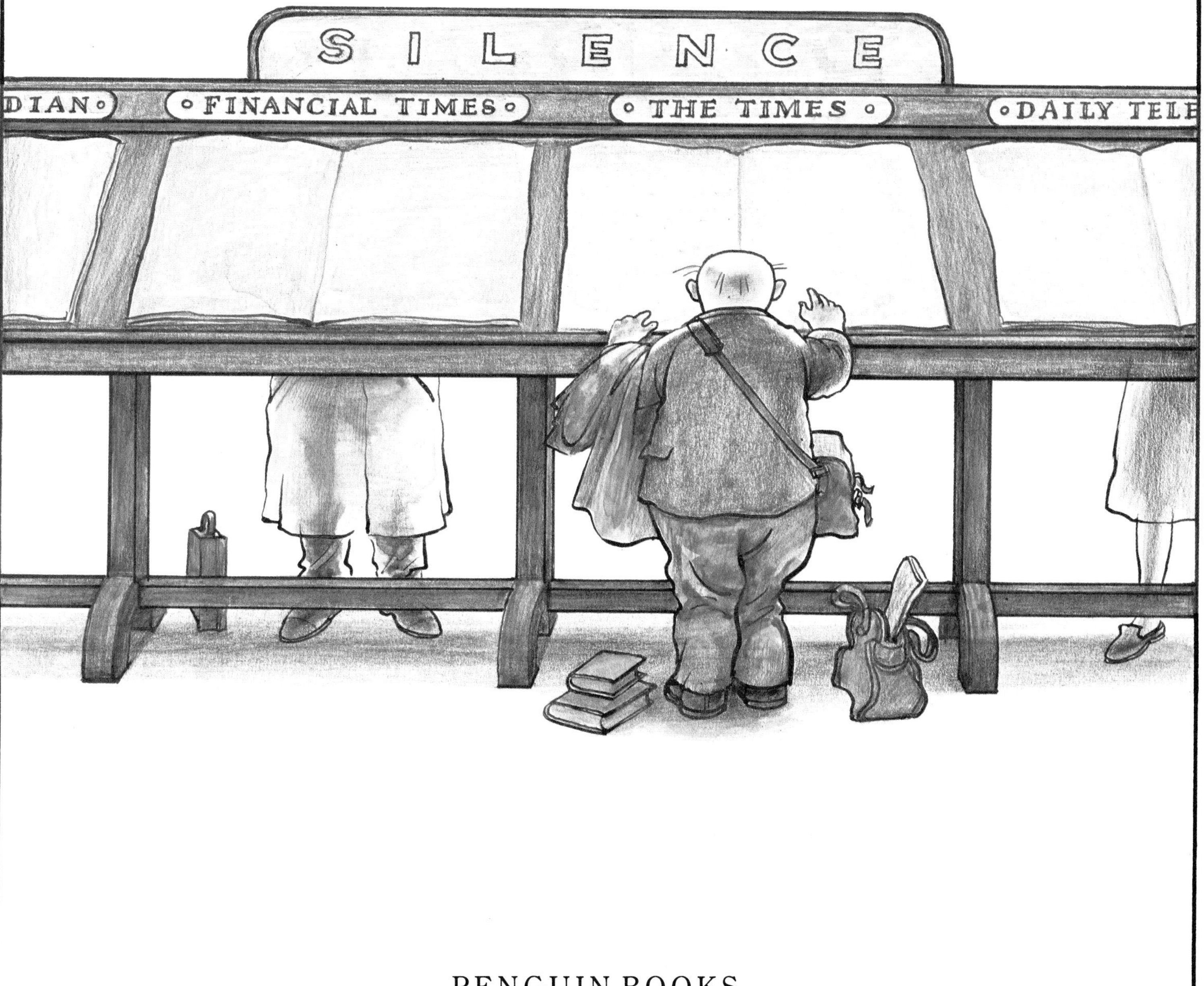
SILENCE
DIAN
FINANCIAL TIMES
THE TIMES
DAILY TELE

PENGUIN BOOKS
London

PENGUIN BOOKS

Published by the Penguin Group
Penguin Books Ltd, 27 Wrights Lane, London W8 5TZ, England
Penguin Books USA Inc., 375 Hudson Street, New York, New York 10014, USA
Penguin Books Australia Ltd, Ringwood, Victoria, Australia
Penguin Books Canada Ltd, 10 Alcorn Avenue, Toronto, Ontario, Canada, M4V 3B2
Penguin Books (NZ) Ltd, 182-190 Wairau Road, Auckland 10, New Zealand

Penguin Books Ltd, Registered Offices: Harmondsworth, Middlesex, England

First published in Great Britain by Hamish Hamilton Ltd 1982
First published in the United States of America
by Schocken Books 1982
Published in Penguin Books 1983
13 15 17 19 20 18 16 14

Printed and bound in Singapore by Kyodo Printing Co

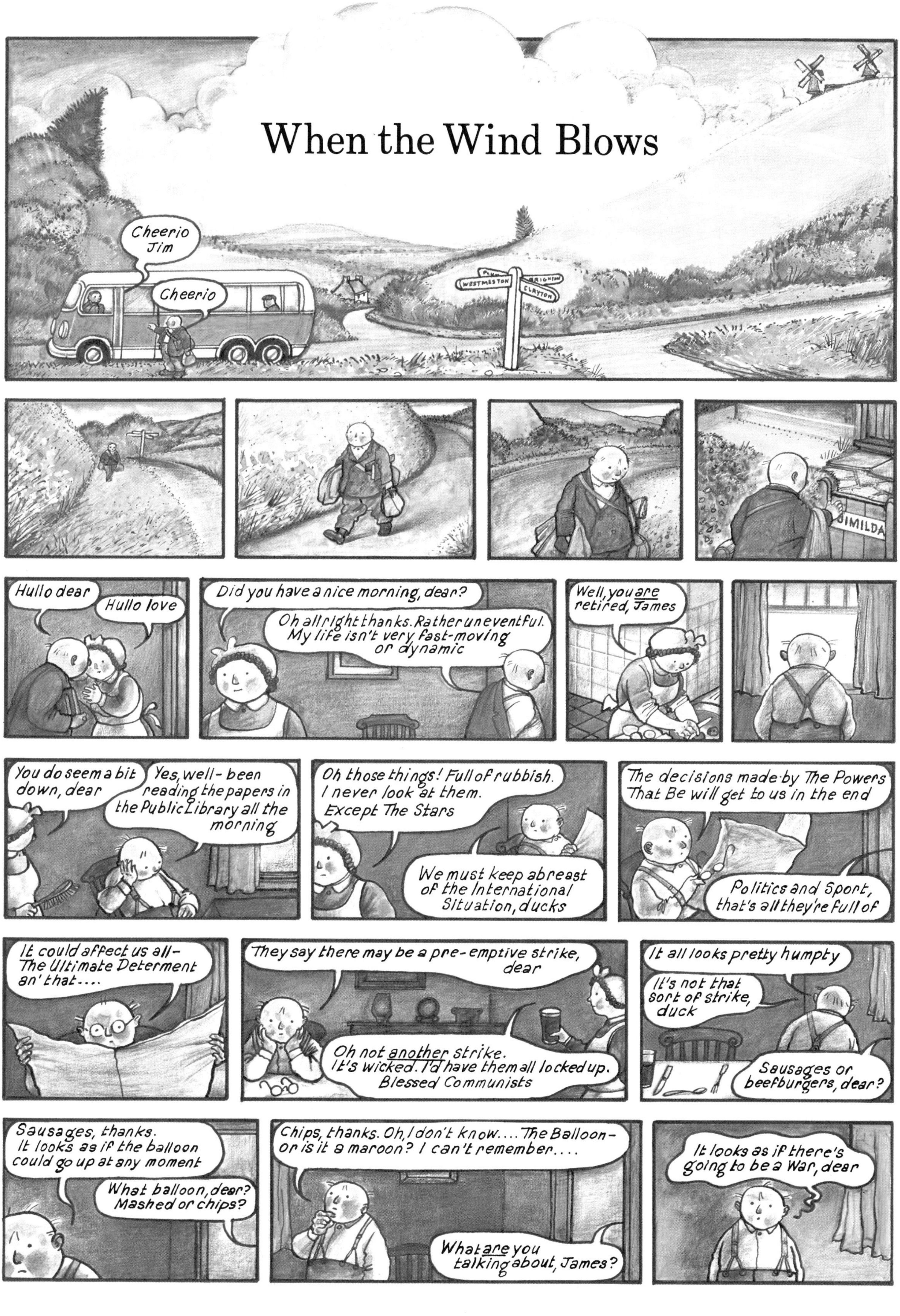
When the Wind Blows
Cheerio Jim
Cheerio
WESTMESTON
BRIGHTON
CLAYTON
JIMILDA
Hullo dear
Hullo love
Did you have a nice morning, dear?
Oh all right thanks. Rather uneventful. My life isn't very fast-moving or dynamic
Well, you are retired, James
You do seem a bit down, dear
Yes, well- been reading the papers in the Public Library all the morning
Oh those things! Full of rubbish. I never look at them. Except The Stars
We must keep abreast of the International Situation, ducks
The decisions made by The Powers That Be will get to us in the end
Politics and Sport, that's all they're full of
It could affect us all- The Ultimate Determent an' that....
They say there may be a pre-emptive strike, dear
Oh not another strike. It's wicked. I'd have them all locked up. Blessed Communists
It all looks pretty humpty
It's not that sort of strike, duck
Sausages or beefburgers, dear?
Sausages, thanks. It looks as if the balloon could go up at any moment
What balloon, dear? Mashed or chips?
Chips, thanks. Oh, I don't know.... The Balloon- or is it a maroon? I can't remember....
What are you talking about, James?
It looks as if there's going to be a War, dear

Yes, they say it might break out at any time now
Well, at least _you_ won't be called up, James

You're far too old

Thank you, my beloved. I'm still two years younger than you

Well, if the worst comes to the worst, we'll just have to roll up our sleeves, tighten our belts and put on our tin hats till it's VE day again

It won't be like that this time, love

I think this one is called The Big Bang Theory

It's all been worked out by brilliant scientists

Well, we survived the last one. We can do it again. It'll take more than a few bombs to get me down

Yes, we must always look on the bright side, ducks

Nice dinner, dear

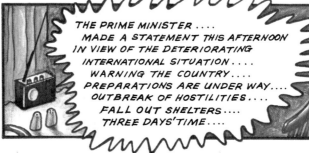
THE PRIME MINISTER.... MADE A STATEMENT THIS AFTERNOON IN VIEW OF THE DETERIORATING INTERNATIONAL SITUATION.... WARNING THE COUNTRY.... PREPARATIONS ARE UNDER WAY.... OUTBREAK OF HOSTILITIES.... FALL OUT SHELTERS.... THREE DAYS' TIME....

CRUMBS!

What's the matter, dear? Have you burned yourself?

This is it, ducks! This is really it!

Another sausage, dear?

I shouldn't worry too much. It'll probably all blow over

Three days! Blimey! Three days!

Language, James! Language!

Crumbs! It's lucky I got more leaflets from the Public Library only this morning.

Here we are - see? "THE HOUSEHOLDER'S GUIDE TO SURVIVAL"

This one should be really authoritative. It's printed by the County Council.

We'd better commence the construction of the Fall Out Shelter immediately, dear. We must do the correct thing

There's treacle tart and custard or cold bread and butter pudding....

Treacle tart, please

Fall Out? I thought they did that in the Army?

No dear, it's Fall _In_ in the Army - Fall In

Thank Goodness I got those Official Leaflets today. Suppose I hadn't! We'd have been totally non-prepared! Just think!

Do you have to dig a hole, like the old Andersons in the War?

Oh no, dear. That's all old-fashioned. With modern scientific methods you just use doors with cushions and books on top

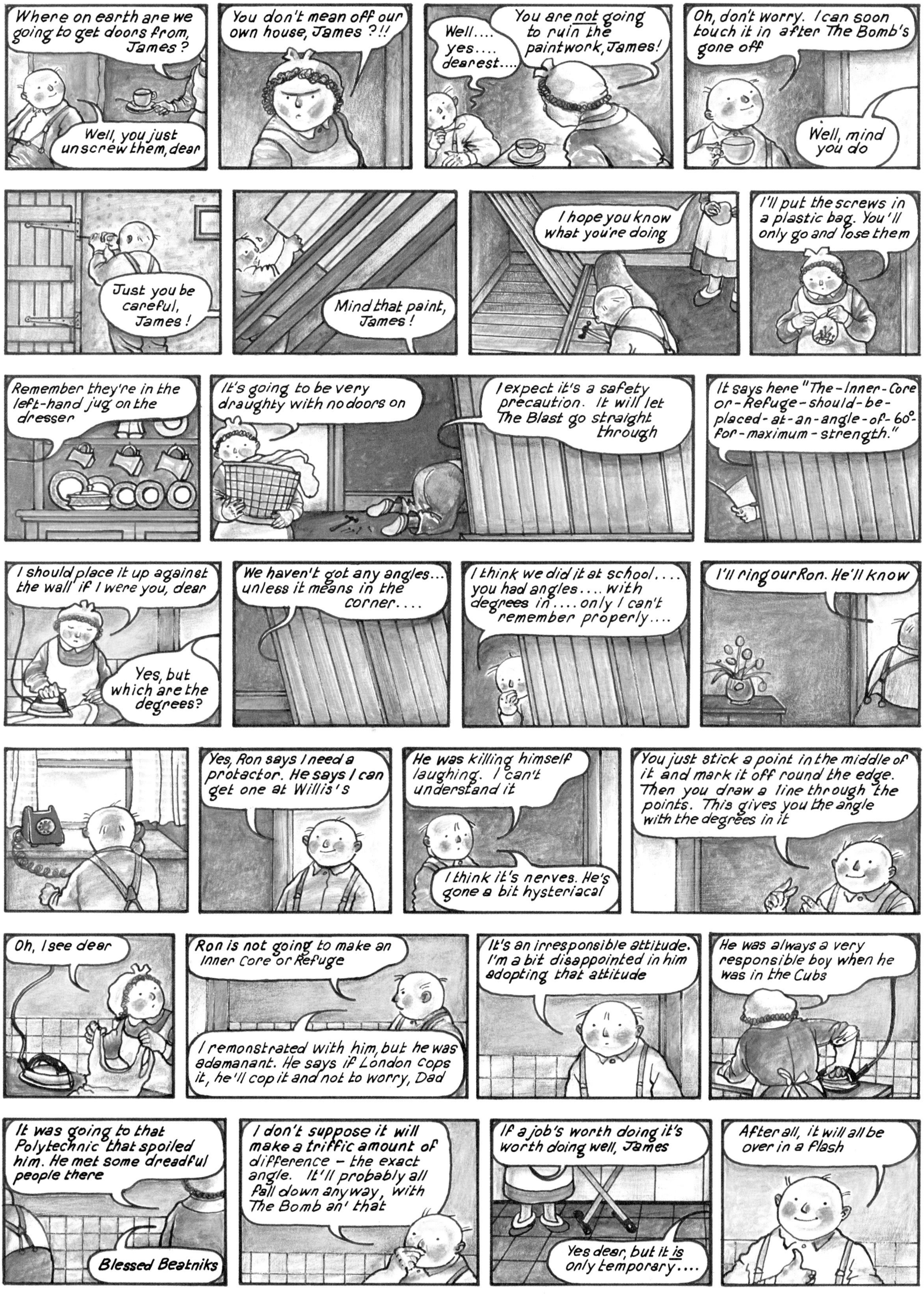
Where on earth are we going to get doors from, James?
Well, you just unscrew them, dear
You don't mean off our own house, James?!!
Well.... yes.... dearest....
You are not going to ruin the paintwork, James!
Oh, don't worry. I can soon touch it in after The Bomb's gone off
Well, mind you do
Just you be careful, James!
Mind that paint, James!
I hope you know what you're doing
I'll put the screws in a plastic bag. You'll only go and lose them
Remember they're in the left-hand jug on the dresser
It's going to be very draughty with no doors on
I expect it's a safety precaution. It will let The Blast go straight through
It says here "The-Inner-Core or-Refuge-should-be-placed-at-an-angle-of-60°-for-maximum-strength."
I should place it up against the wall if I were you, dear
Yes, but which are the degrees?
We haven't got any angles... unless it means in the corner....
I think we did it at school.... you had angles.... with degrees in.... only I can't remember properly....
I'll ring our Ron. He'll know
Yes, Ron says I need a protactor. He says I can get one at Willis's
He was killing himself laughing. I can't understand it
I think it's nerves. He's gone a bit hysteriacal
You just stick a point in the middle of it and mark it off round the edge. Then you draw a line through the points. This gives you the angle with the degrees in it
Oh, I see dear
Ron is not going to make an Inner Core or Refuge
I remonstrated with him, but he was adamanant. He says if London cops it, he'll cop it and not to worry, Dad
It's an irresponsible attitude. I'm a bit disappointed in him adopting that attitude
He was always a very responsible boy when he was in the Cubs
It was going to that Polytechnic that spoiled him. He met some dreadful people there
Blessed Beatniks
I don't suppose it will make a triffic amount of difference – the exact angle. It'll probably all fall down anyway, with The Bomb an' that
If a job's worth doing it's worth doing well, James
Yes dear, but it is only temporary....
After all, it will all be over in a flash

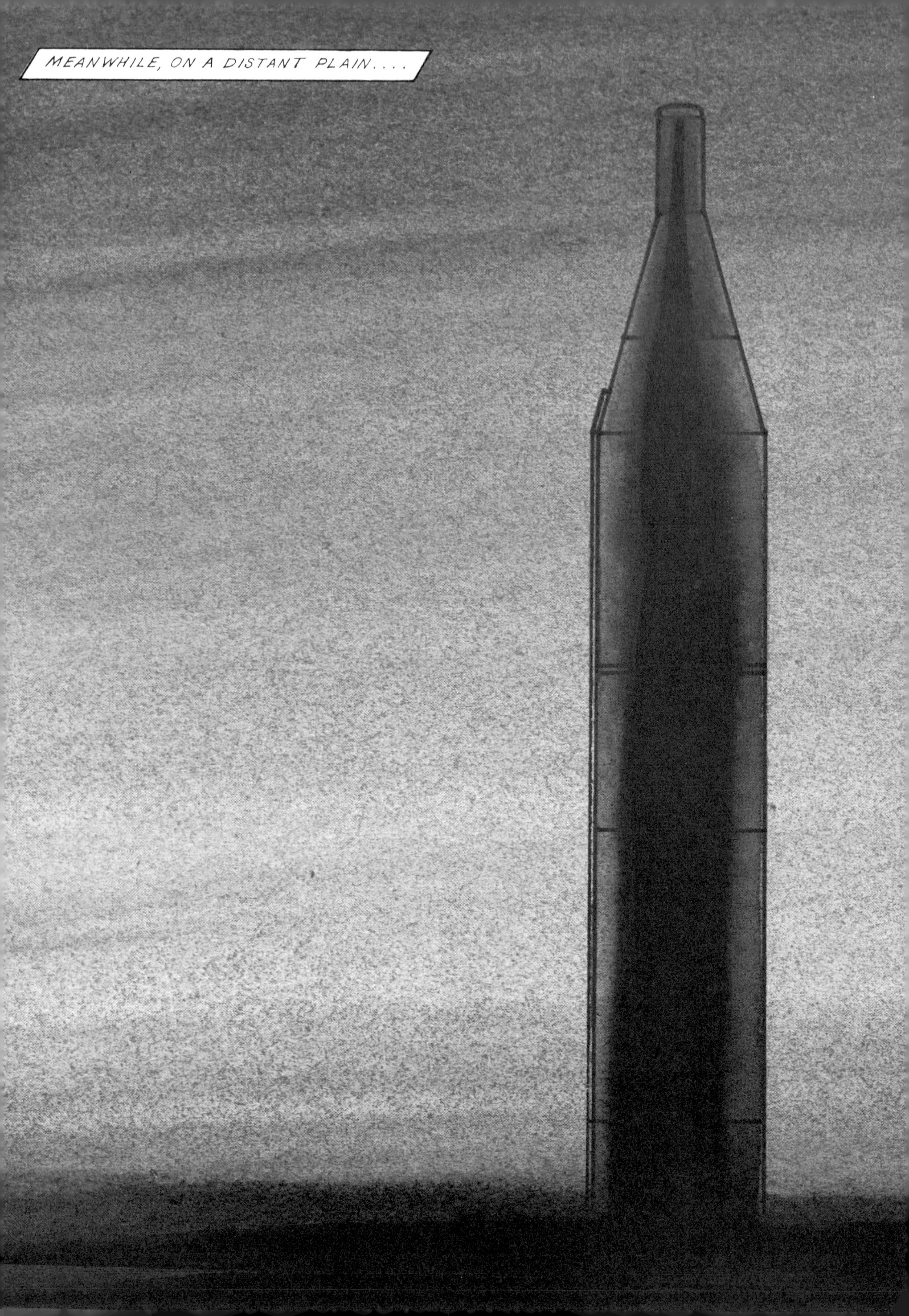
MEANWHILE, ON A DISTANT PLAIN....

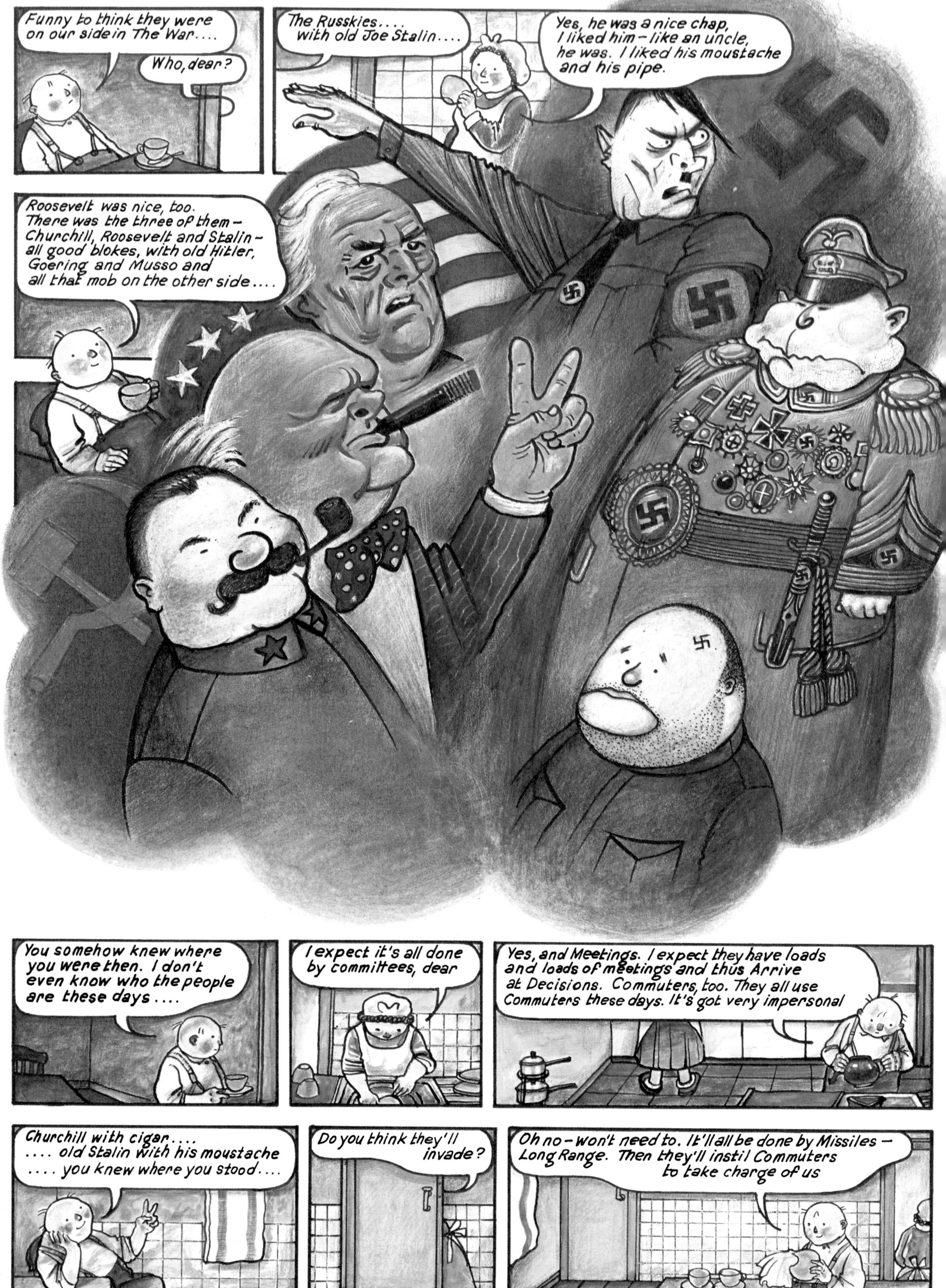

Funny to think they were on our side in The War....
Who, dear?
The Russkies.... with old Joe Stalin....
Yes, he was a nice chap, I liked him – like an uncle, he was. I liked his moustache and his pipe.
Roosevelt was nice, too. There was the three of them – Churchill, Roosevelt and Stalin – all good blokes, with old Hitler, Goering and Musso and all that mob on the other side....
You somehow knew where you were then. I don't even know who the people are these days....
I expect it's all done by committees, dear
Yes, and Meetings. I expect they have loads and loads of meetings and thus Arrive at Decisions. Commuters, too. They all use Commuters these days. It's got very impersonal
Churchill with cigar.... .... old Stalin with his moustache .... you knew where you stood....
Do you think they'll invade?
Oh no – won't need to. It'll all be done by Missiles – Long Range. Then they'll instil Commuters to take charge of us

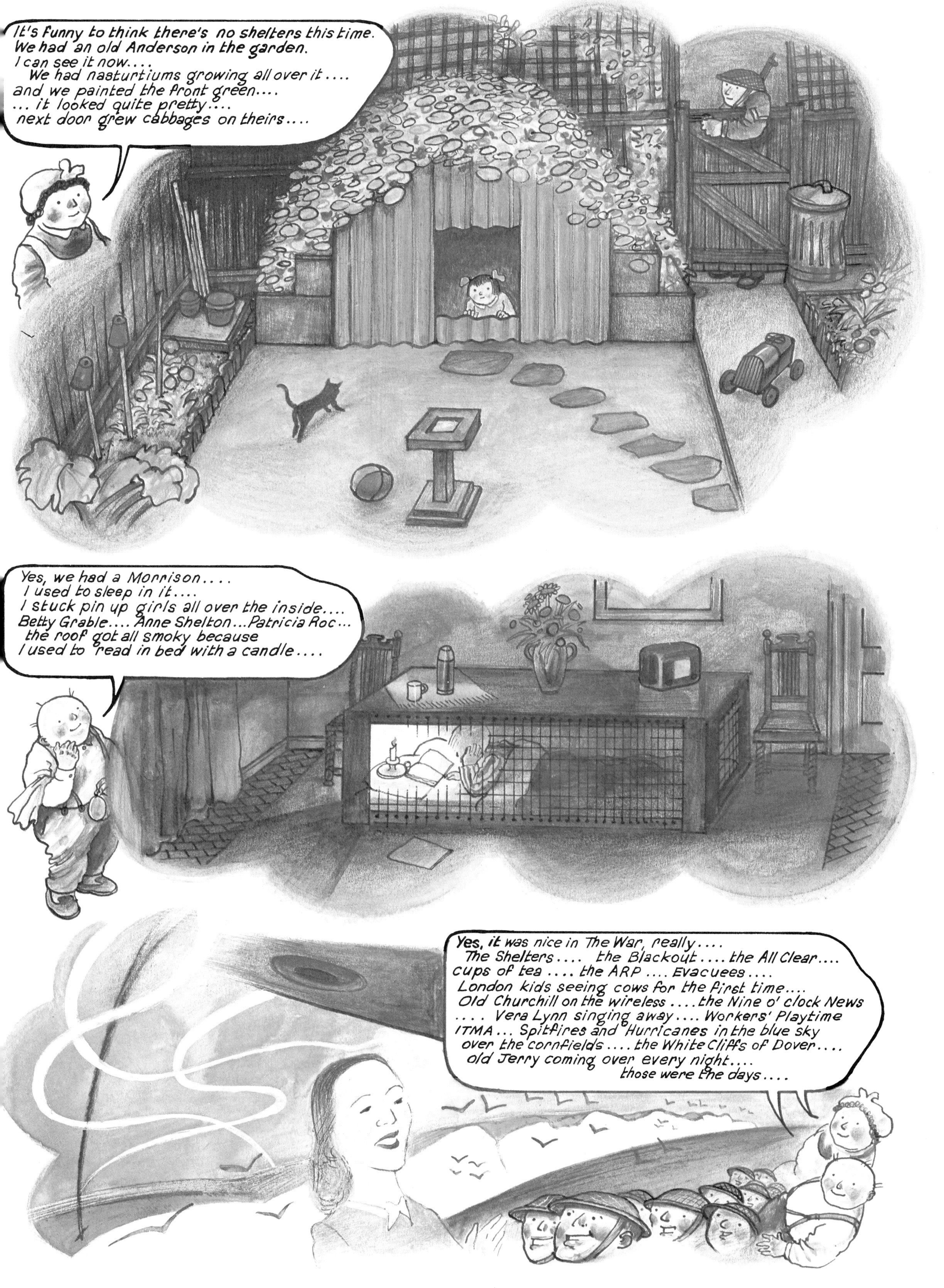
It's funny to think there's no shelters this time. We had an old Anderson in the garden. I can see it now.... We had nasturtiums growing all over it.... and we painted the front green.... ... it looked quite pretty.... next door grew cabbages on theirs....
Yes, we had a Morrison.... I used to sleep in it.... I stuck pin up girls all over the inside.... Betty Grable.... Anne Shelton...Patricia Roc... the roof got all smoky because I used to read in bed with a candle....
Yes, it was nice in The War, really.... The Shelters.... the Blackout.... the All Clear.... cups of tea.... the ARP.... Evacuees.... London kids seeing cows for the first time.... Old Churchill on the wireless.... the Nine o' clock News .... Vera Lynn singing away.... Workers' Playtime ITMA... Spitfires and Hurricanes in the blue sky over the cornfields.... the White Cliffs of Dover.... old Jerry coming over every night.... those were the days....

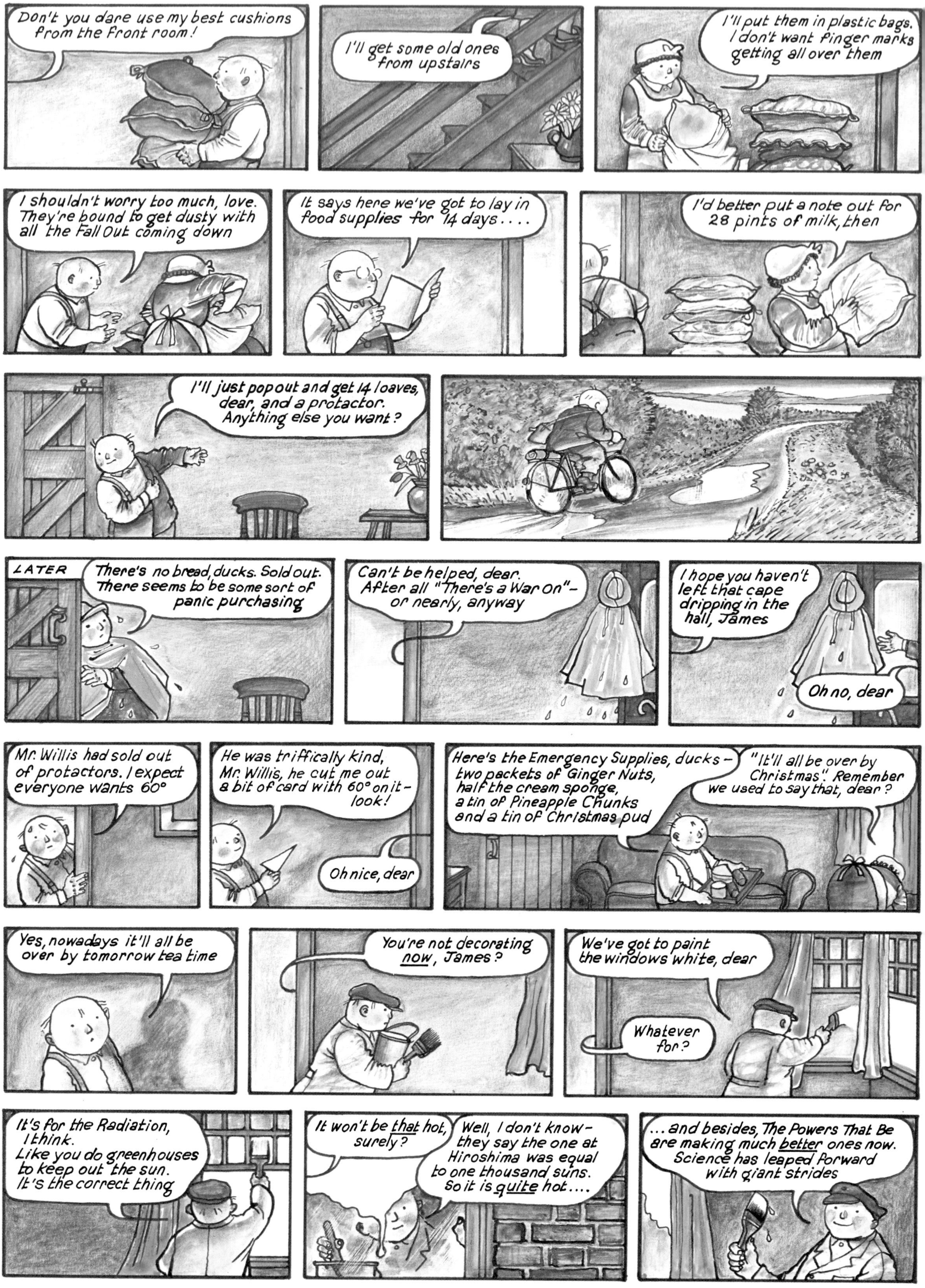
Don't you dare use my best cushions from the front room!
I'll get some old ones from upstairs
I'll put them in plastic bags. I don't want finger marks getting all over them
I shouldn't worry too much, love. They're bound to get dusty with all the Fall Out coming down
It says here we've got to lay in food supplies for 14 days....
I'd better put a note out for 28 pints of milk, then
I'll just pop out and get 14 loaves, dear, and a protactor. Anything else you want?
LATER
There's no bread, ducks. Sold out. There seems to be some sort of panic purchasing
Can't be helped, dear. After all "There's a War On" – or nearly, anyway
I hope you haven't left that cape dripping in the hall, James
Oh no, dear
Mr. Willis had sold out of protactors. I expect everyone wants 60°
He was trifficaly kind, Mr. Willis, he cut me out a bit of card with 60° on it – look!
Oh nice, dear
Here's the Emergency Supplies, ducks – two packets of Ginger Nuts, half the cream sponge, a tin of Pineapple Chunks and a tin of Christmas pud
"It'll all be over by Christmas". Remember we used to say that, dear?
Yes, nowadays it'll all be over by tomorrow tea time
You're not decorating now, James?
We've got to paint the windows white, dear
Whatever for?
It's for the Radiation, I think. Like you do greenhouses to keep out the sun. It's the correct thing
It won't be that hot, surely?
Well, I don't know – they say the one at Hiroshima was equal to one thousand suns. So it is quite hot....
...and besides, The Powers That Be are making much better ones now. Science has leaped forward with giant strides

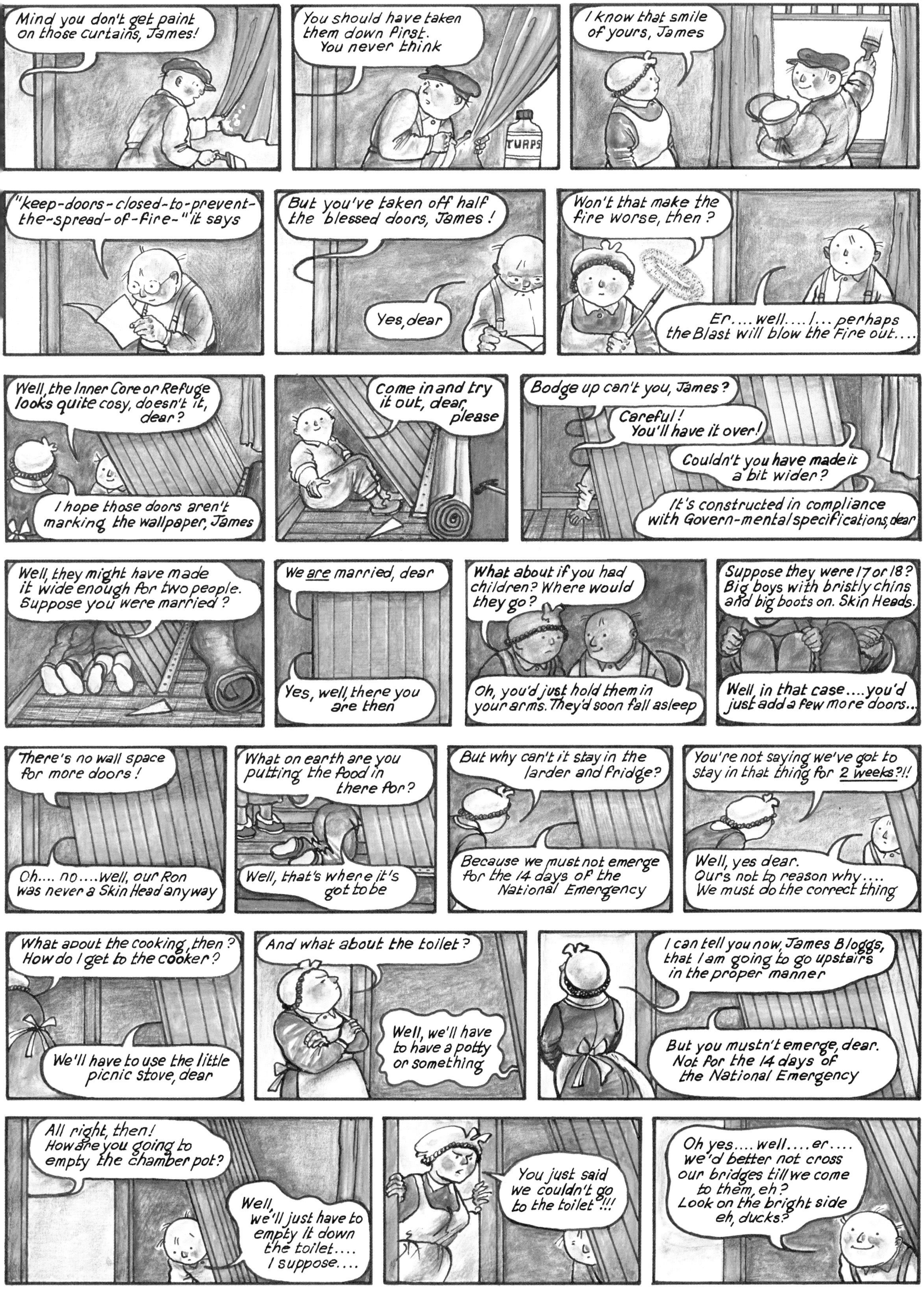
Mind you don't get paint on those curtains, James!
You should have taken them down first. You never think
I know that smile of yours, James
TURPS
"keep-doors-closed-to-prevent-the-spread-of-fire-" it says
But you've taken off half the blessed doors, James!
Yes, dear
Won't that make the fire worse, then?
Er.... well.... I... perhaps the Blast will blow the Fire out....
Well, the Inner Core or Refuge looks quite cosy, doesn't it, dear?
I hope those doors aren't marking the wallpaper, James
Come in and try it out, dear, please
Bodge up can't you, James?
Careful! You'll have it over!
Couldn't you have made it a bit wider?
It's constructed in compliance with Govern-mental specifications, dear
Well, they might have made it wide enough for two people. Suppose you were married?
We are married, dear
Yes, well, there you are then
What about if you had children? Where would they go?
Oh, you'd just hold them in your arms. They'd soon fall asleep
Suppose they were 17 or 18? Big boys with bristly chins and big boots on. Skin Heads.
Well in that case.... you'd just add a few more doors...
There's no wall space for more doors!
Oh.... no.... well, our Ron was never a Skin Head anyway
What on earth are you putting the food in there for?
Well, that's where it's got to be
But why can't it stay in the larder and fridge?
Because we must not emerge for the 14 days of the National Emergency
You're not saying we've got to stay in that thing for 2 weeks?!!
Well, yes dear. Ours not to reason why.... We must do the correct thing
What about the cooking, then? How do I get to the cooker?
We'll have to use the little picnic stove, dear
And what about the toilet?
Well, we'll have to have a potty or something
I can tell you now, James Bloggs, that I am going to go upstairs in the proper manner
But you mustn't emerge, dear. Not for the 14 days of the National Emergency
All right, then! How are you going to empty the chamber pot?
Well, we'll just have to empty it down the toilet.... I suppose....
You just said we couldn't go to the toilet!!!
Oh yes.... well.... er.... we'd better not cross our bridges till we come to them, eh? Look on the bright side eh, ducks?

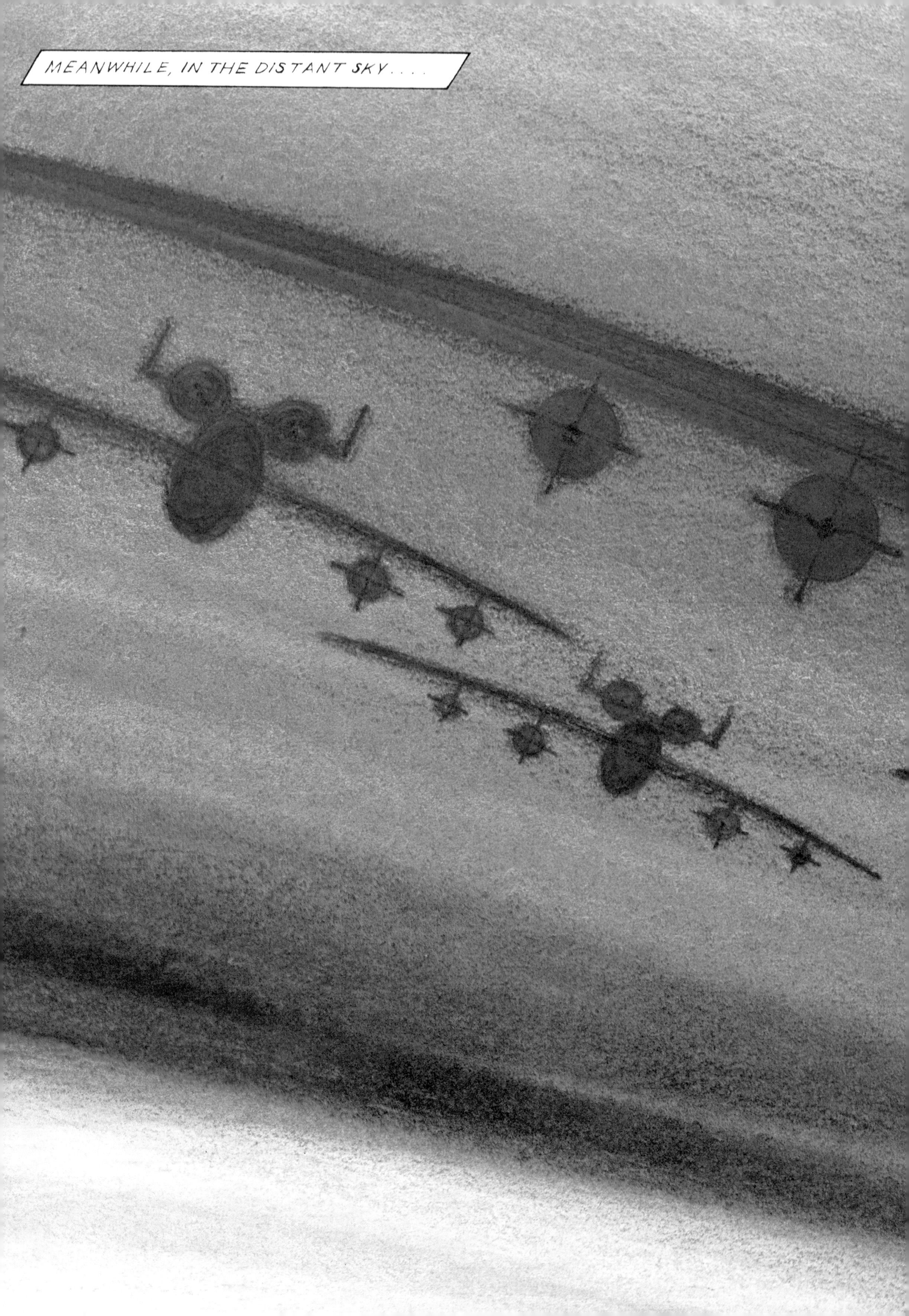
MEANWHILE, IN THE DISTANT SKY....

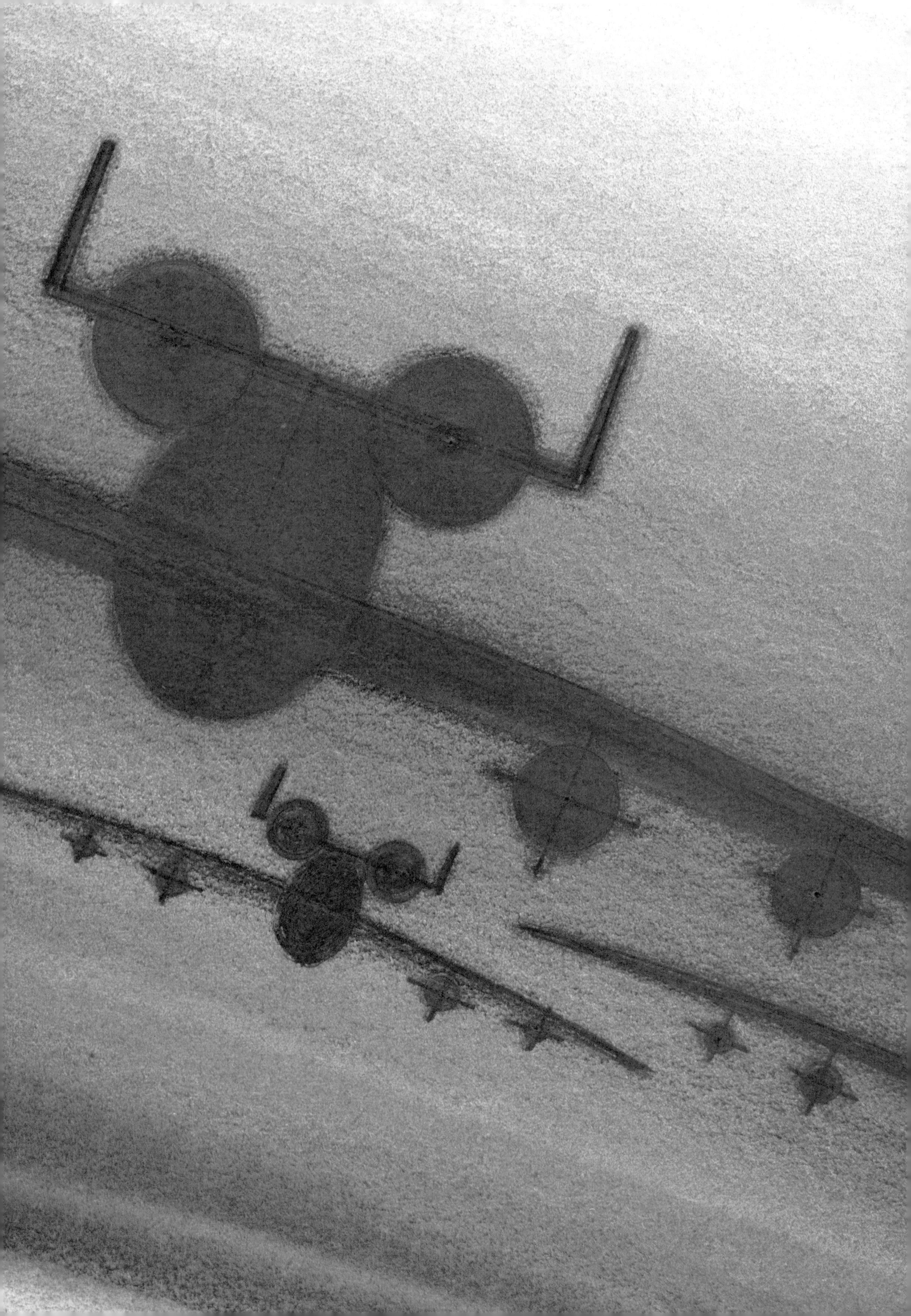

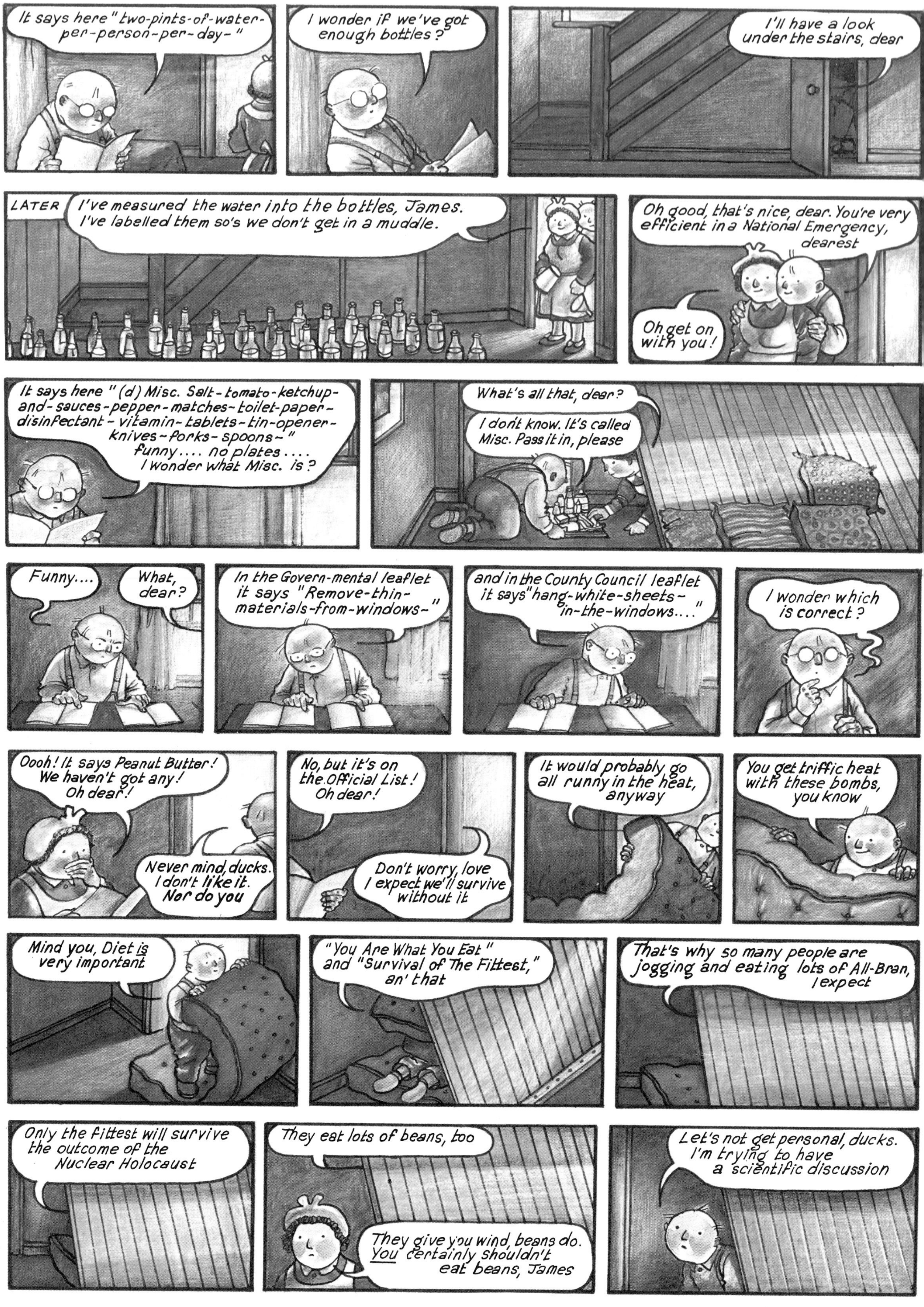
It says here "two-pints-of-water-per-person-per-day-"
I wonder if we've got enough bottles?
I'll have a look under the stairs, dear
LATER
I've measured the water into the bottles, James. I've labelled them so's we don't get in a muddle.
Oh good, that's nice, dear. You're very efficient in a National Emergency, dearest
Oh get on with you!
It says here "(d) Misc. Salt-tomato-ketchup-and-sauces-pepper-matches-toilet-paper-disinfectant-vitamin-tablets-tin-opener-knives-forks-spoons-" funny.... no plates.... I wonder what Misc. is?
What's all that, dear?
I don't know. It's called Misc. Pass it in, please
Funny....
What, dear?
In the Govern-mental leaflet it says "Remove-thin-materials-from-windows-"
and in the County Council leaflet it says "hang-white-sheets-in-the-windows...."
I wonder which is correct?
Oooh! It says Peanut Butter! We haven't got any! Oh dear!
Never mind, ducks. I don't like it. Nor do you
No, but it's on the Official List! Oh dear!
Don't worry, love I expect we'll survive without it
It would probably go all runny in the heat, anyway
You get triffic heat with these bombs, you know
Mind you, Diet is very important
"You Are What You Eat" and "Survival of The Fittest," an' that
That's why so many people are jogging and eating lots of All-Bran, I expect
Only the fittest will survive the outcome of the Nuclear Holocaust
They eat lots of beans, too
They give you wind, beans do. You certainly shouldn't eat beans, James
Let's not get personal, ducks. I'm trying to have a scientific discussion

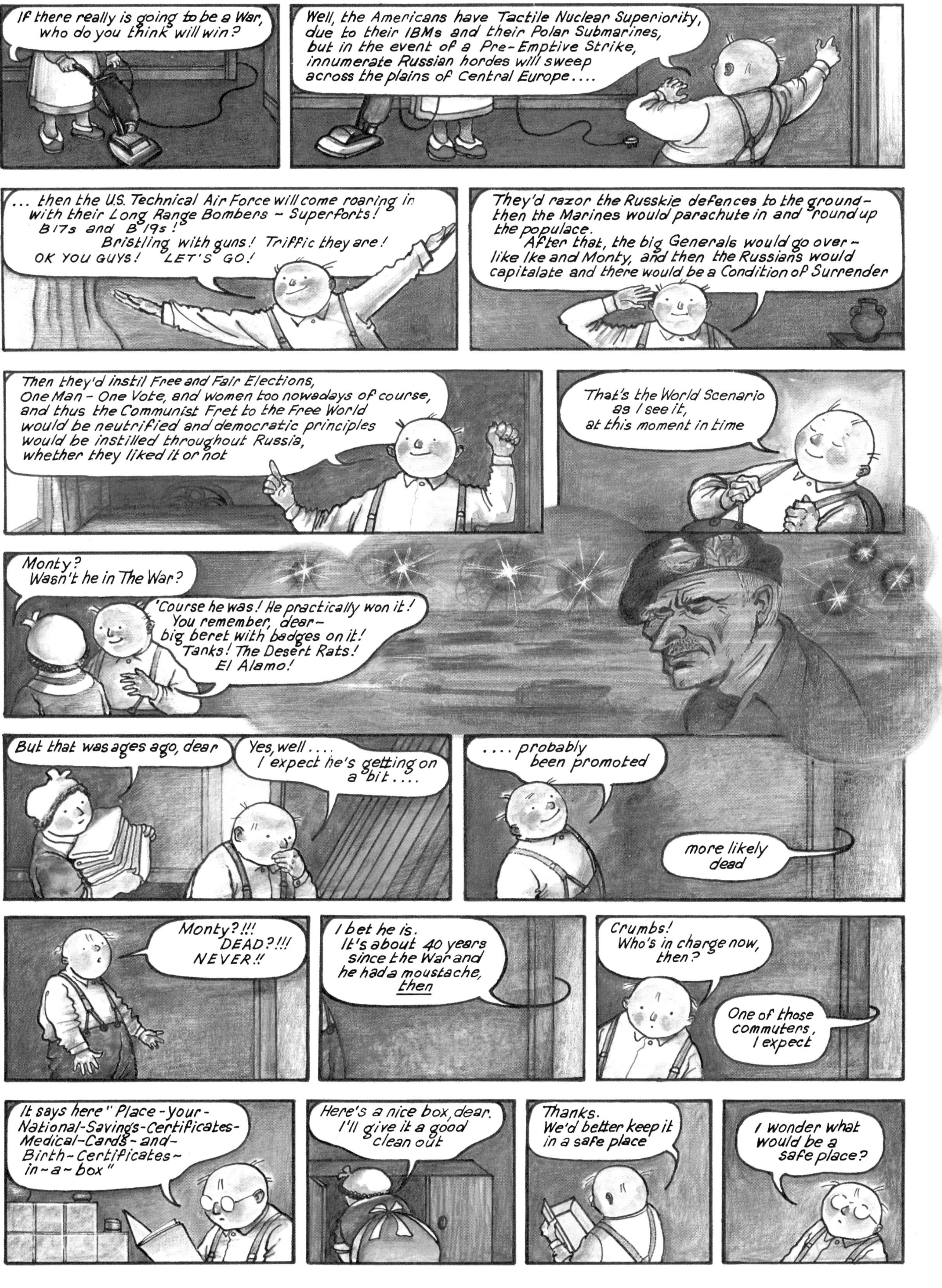
If there really is going to be a War, who do you think will win?
Well, the Americans have Tactile Nuclear Superiority, due to their IBMs and their Polar Submarines, but in the event of a Pre-Emptive Strike, innumerate Russian hordes will sweep across the plains of Central Europe....
... then the U.S. Technical Air Force will come roaring in with their Long Range Bombers - Superforts! B17s and B19s! Bristling with guns! Triffic they are! OK YOU GUYS! LET'S GO!
They'd razor the Russkie defences to the ground - then the Marines would parachute in and round up the populace. After that, the big Generals would go over - like Ike and Monty, and then the Russians would capitalate and there would be a Condition of Surrender
Then they'd instil Free and Fair Elections, One Man - One Vote, and women too nowadays of course, and thus the Communist Fret to the Free World would be neutrified and democratic principles would be instilled throughout Russia, whether they liked it or not
That's the World Scenario as I see it, at this moment in time
Monty? Wasn't he in The War?
'Course he was! He practically won it! You remember, dear - big beret with badges on it! Tanks! The Desert Rats! El Alamo!
But that was ages ago, dear
Yes, well .... I expect he's getting on a bit....
.... probably been promoted
more likely dead
Monty?!!! DEAD?!!! NEVER!!
I bet he is. It's about 40 years since the War and he had a moustache, then
Crumbs! Who's in charge now, then?
One of those commuters, I expect
It says here "Place-your-National-Savings-Certificates-Medical-Cards-and-Birth-Certificates-in-a-box"
Here's a nice box, dear. I'll give it a good clean out
Thanks. We'd better keep it in a safe place
I wonder what would be a safe place?

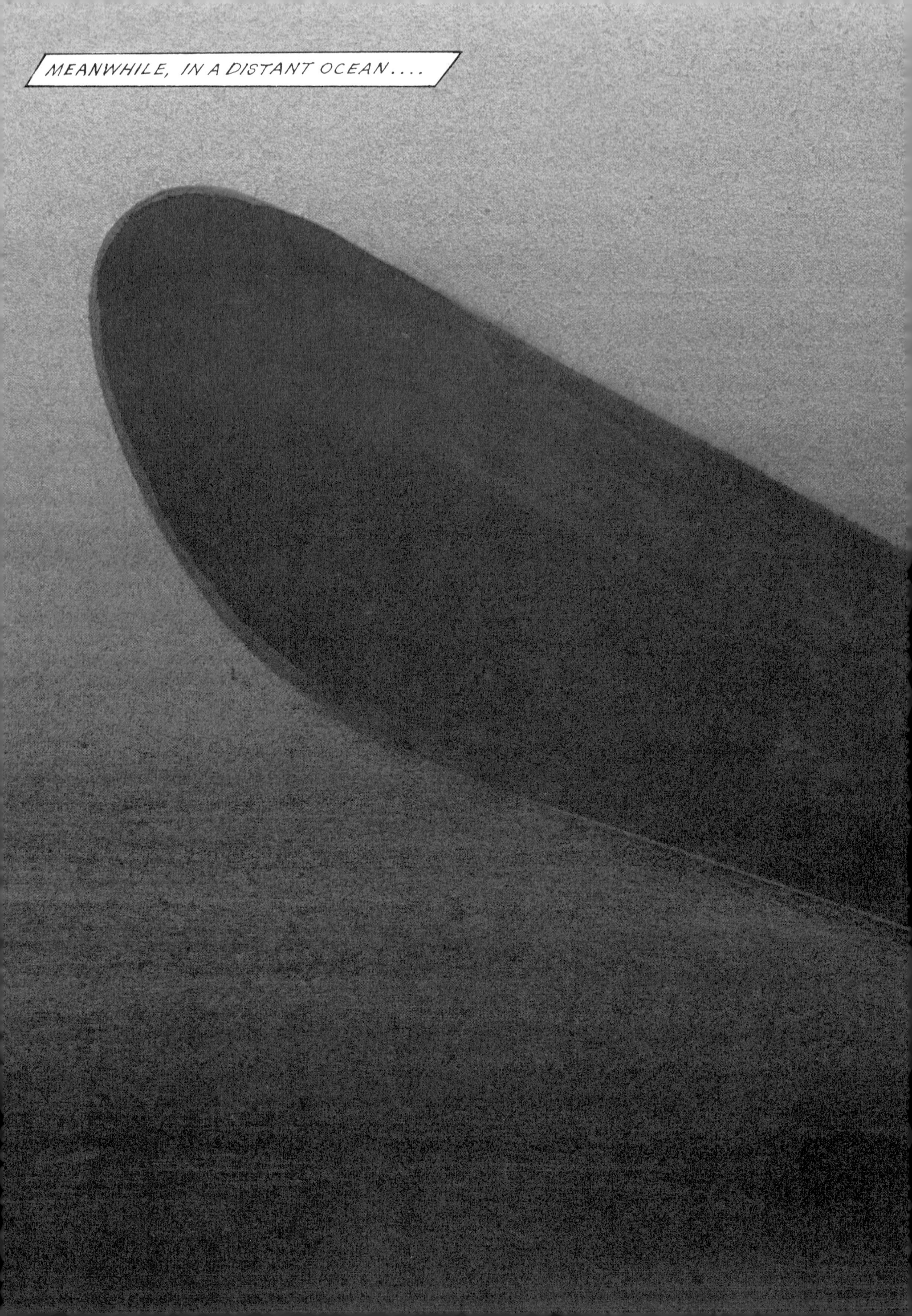
MEANWHILE, IN A DISTANT OCEAN....

Who's in charge of the Russians, dear?

Oh.... er .... it's Shivinski, isn't it? Or Molotov.... no, Molotov is just a cocktail, I think.
Kruschev! Yes! That's right! He bangs his shoe - B and K - Bulgaria and Kruschev! That's them.
And that bloke Marks has got something to do with it.

What are you doing, dear?

Blocking up the window in compliance with the Govern-mental Directive. It's the correct thing

Yes, then there's the usual Committee, of course.
The Commontern, they call it - the Soviet Supreme - they're in charge of the B.J. Key - that's the Secret Service - S.S. for short.
Our lot is called E.M.I. 5 - it's all very complicated, ducks

Well, mind you don't scratch the polish

Is it any good writing him a letter, do you think?

Who?

This leader - B.J. Whatsisname?

What are you going to say, dear?

Oh, I don't know - er - Dear Sir, Mr. B.J. Thing...er... we the people of Britain are fed up with being bombed we had enough of it last time with old Hitler so will you just leave us in peace you live your life and we'll live ours hope you are well....

... please don't drop any bombs Yours Sincerely Mr. and Mrs. J. Bloggs

Very good, dear, very nice. It might be a bit late for the post. You know what the post is like these days

First Class might just get there.... but I must just do this list - "dust-bin-calendar-books - games - paper - pencils - shovel - spade - crowbar - axe - hatchet - saw - whistle - and/or - gong - (for - alarms) - suit cases - for - furniture - of - evacuation - string - pliers -

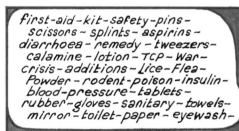

first-aid-kit-safety-pins- scissors - splints - aspirins - diarrhoea - remedy - tweezers - calamine - lotion - TCP - War- crisis - additions - Lice-Flea- Powder - rodent-poison-insulin- blood-pressure-tablets - rubber-gloves - sanitary - towels- mirror - toilet-paper - eyewash -

I wonder if it's true about the paper bags? Or is it just a joke?

I never know if it's a joke or not....

What's that, dear?

Well, they say you should get into a paper bag just before The Bomb goes off

Whatever for?

I suppose it's like the white paint - it deflects the heat a bit

Sounds silly to me

There are some paper bags.... We had the spuds from the farm in them.... there should be four....

They'll be filthy, James

Are you sure that bag is clean, James?

Yes, dear. I cleaned it thoroughly

You do look silly

I wonder if it's all right to have eye holes?

They say it's the correct thing to wear white. People in Hiroshima with patterned clothes got burned where the pattern was, and not so much on the white bits - even the buttons showed up

Yes, but they were Japanese

!!?

Is there a clean white shirt, dear? Ready for The Bomb?

You're not going to wear that nice new one I gave you for Christmas! I don't want that spoiled

You can wear your old clothes for The Bomb and save your best for afterwards

All right, dear. But is there an old <u>white</u> one? Without stripes. I don't want stripes all over me

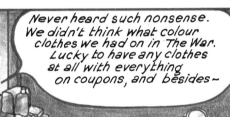

Never heard such nonsense. We didn't think what colour clothes we had on in The War. Lucky to have any clothes at all with everything on coupons, and besides ~

WE ARE INTERRUPTING THIS PROGRAMME

FOR AN OFFICIAL GOVERNMENT ANNOUNCEMENT

AN ENEMY MISSILE ATTACK HAS BEEN LAUNCHED AGAINST THIS COUNTRY

IN JUST OVER THREE MINUTES

God Almighty, ducks! There's only three minutes to go!!

Oh dear, I'll just get the washing in

COME BACK YOU STUPID FOOL AND GET IN THE SHELTER!

TAKE COVER

How dare you talk to me like that, James!

SHUT UP AND GET IN!

There's no need to forget our manners just because there's a war on

DO NOT LEAVE YOUR HOMES

SHUT UP I'M TRYING TO LISTEN!

STAY INDOORS

I've never heard such language in all my life

DO NOT LEAVE YOUR HOMES

FOR GOD'S SAKE SHUT UP!

LIE DOWN

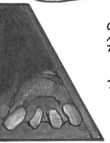

Oh dear! I've left the oven on

GET IN! GET IN! GET IN!

ON NO ACCOUNT TRY TO

The cake will be burned

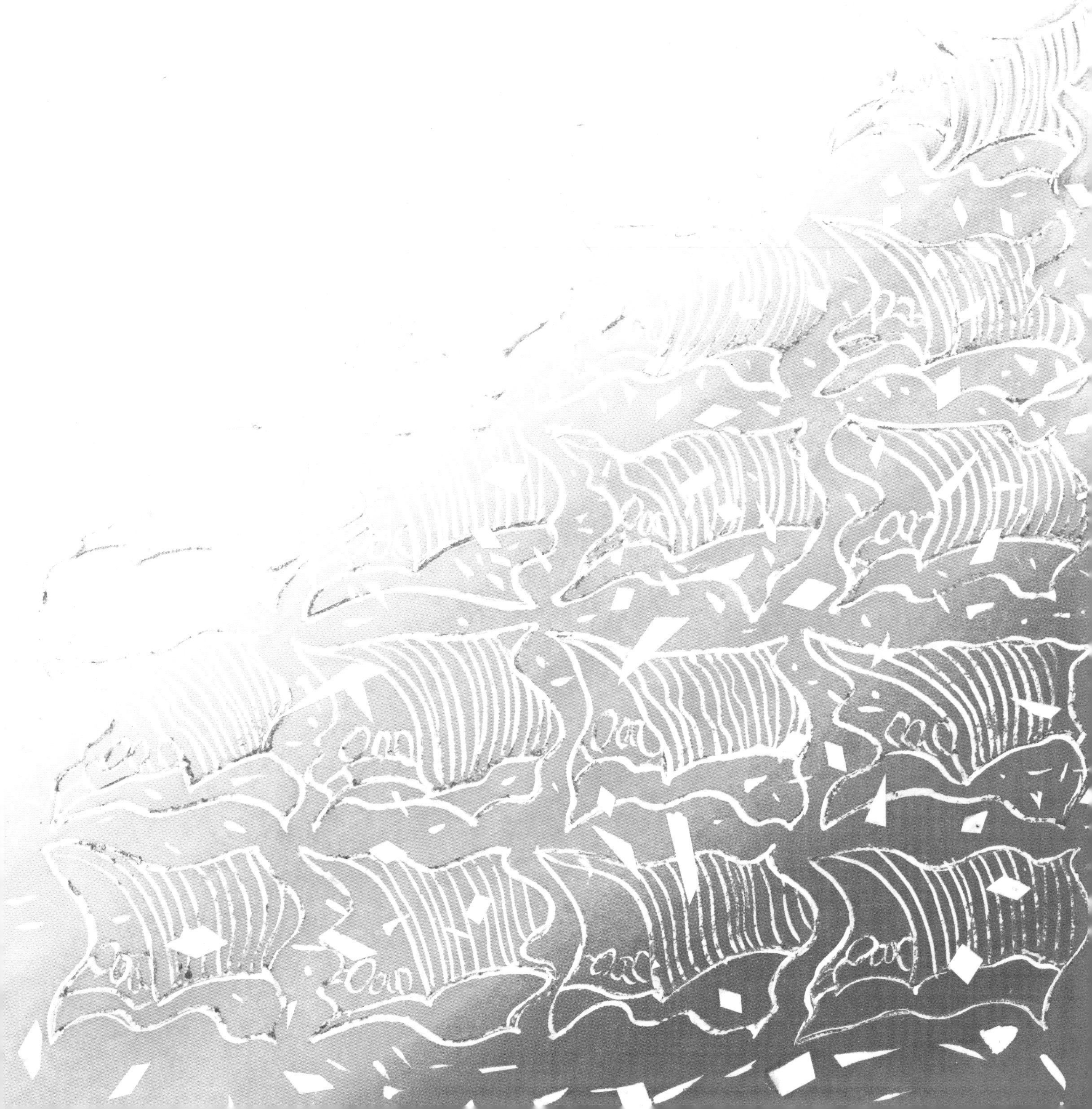

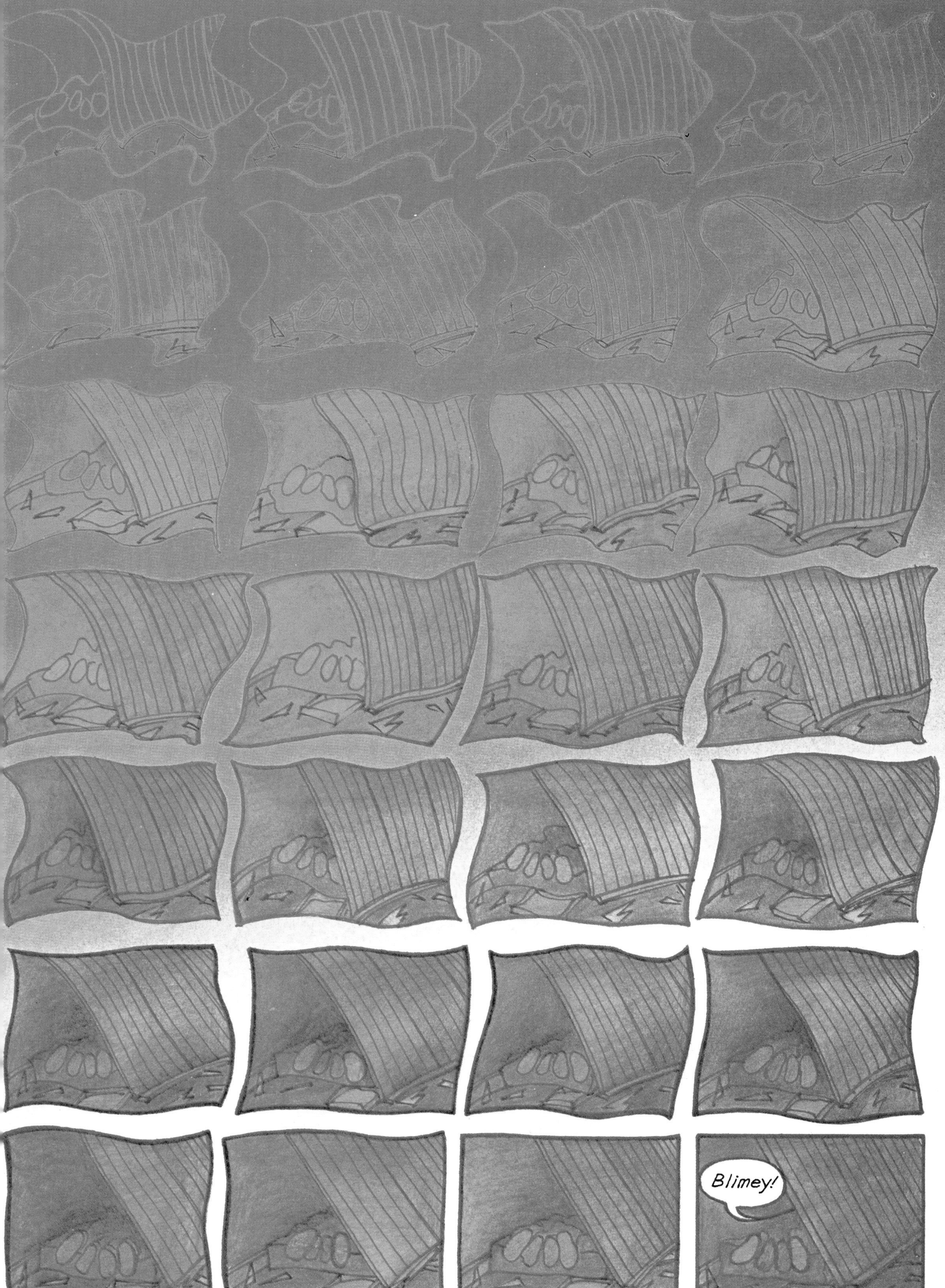
Blimey!

Oooh!
Blimey!
Well I never...
I suppose that was it
I should think so
Blimey!
Are you all right, dear?
Yes thanks, love
Ooh dear! I do feel all shaky....
Never mind, ducks. We're still in one piece, eh?
Yes, I think so....
Wasn't it light?
Yes, triffic. You get triffic light with these bombs
....and the heat..
I know, it's still hot now. Glad I didn't have a striped shirt on
I wonder how far we are from the Epi-centre? .... or was it the Hypo-centre?.... I can't remember....
What's that, dear?
Well, it's the centre of it all – you know – the bull's eye, sort of.... Bang in the middle, or the middle of The Bang, rather....
I should think we were bang in the middle, dear. A Direct Hit – just look at all that glass
No, it couldn't have been a Direct Hit, dear. We would have sustained greater damage and suffered greater casualties
Don't talk to me about damage! Just look at those curtains!
Yes, but it would have been much worse at the Epi – Hypo-Thing, dear
I don't see how it could have been much worse. I'll never get them clean. I'll give them a good soak tonight.
Blessed Germans!
Russkies, dear
The shelter stood up well, didn't it? I constructed it in compliance with Govern – mental specifications
I hope the cushions aren't spoiled
I think some of them blew off in The Blast
I do like nice cushions....
Yes, but there's more important things at the moment, ducks –
.... and curtains. Cushions and curtains

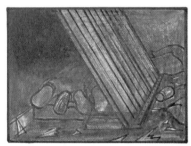

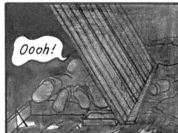

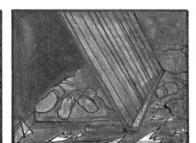

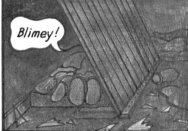

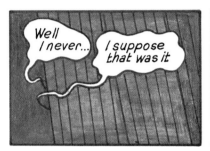

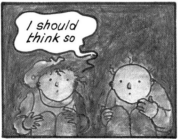

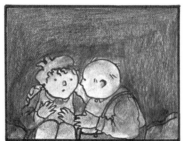

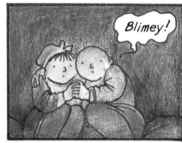

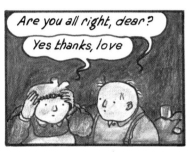

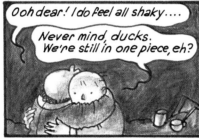

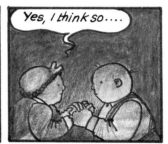

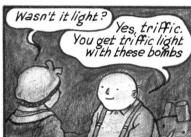

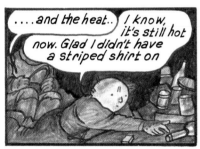

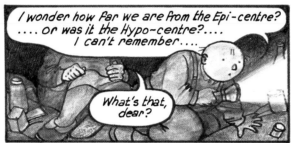

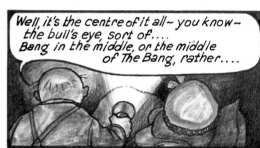

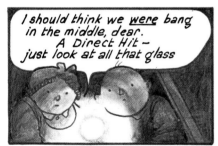

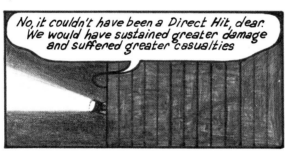

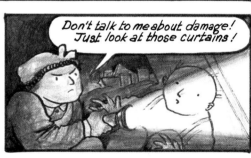

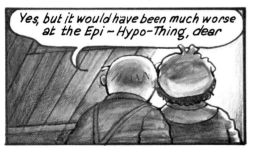

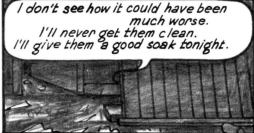

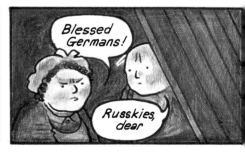

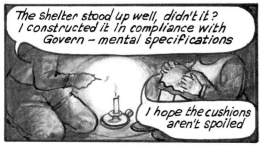

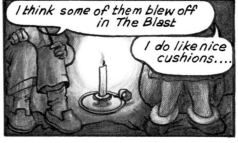

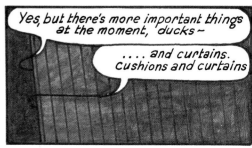

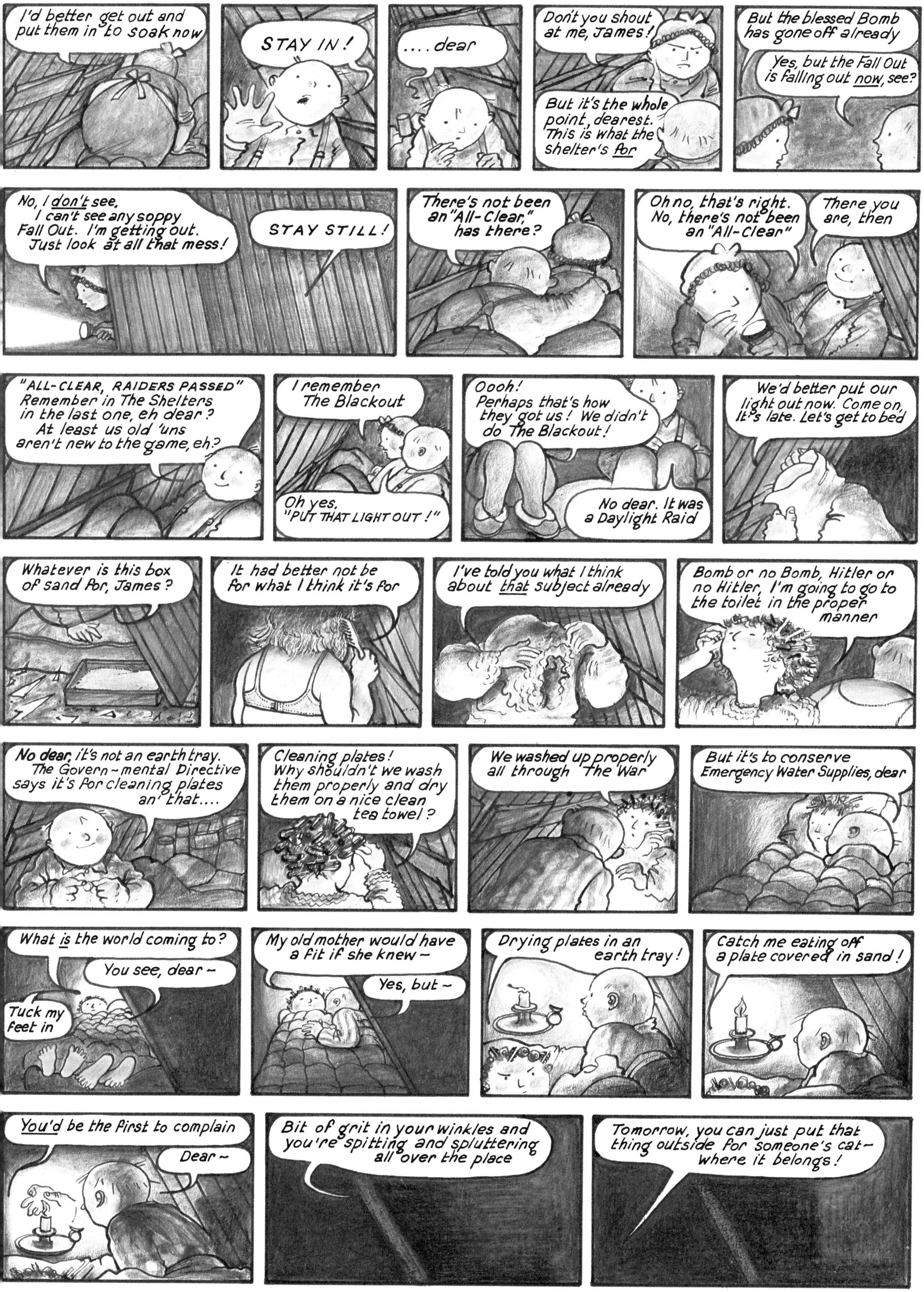

I'd better get out and put them in to soak now
STAY IN!
....dear
Don't you shout at me, James!
But it's the whole point, dearest. This is what the shelter's for
But the blessed Bomb has gone off already
Yes, but the Fall Out is falling out now, see?
No, I don't see. I can't see any soppy Fall Out. I'm getting out. Just look at all that mess!
STAY STILL!
There's not been an "All-Clear," has there?
Oh no, that's right. No, there's not been an "All-Clear"
There you are, then
"ALL-CLEAR, RAIDERS PASSED" Remember in The Shelters in the last one, eh dear? At least us old 'uns aren't new to the game, eh?
I remember The Blackout
Oh yes, "PUT THAT LIGHT OUT!"
Oooh! Perhaps that's how they got us! We didn't do The Blackout!
No dear. It was a Daylight Raid
We'd better put our light out now. Come on, It's late. Let's get to bed
Whatever is this box of sand for, James?
It had better not be for what I think it's for
I've told you what I think about that subject already
Bomb or no Bomb, Hitler or no Hitler, I'm going to go to the toilet in the proper manner
No dear, it's not an earth tray. The Govern-mental Directive says it's for cleaning plates an' that....
Cleaning plates! Why shouldn't we wash them properly and dry them on a nice clean tea towel?
We washed up properly all through The War
But it's to conserve Emergency Water Supplies, dear
What is the world coming to?
You see, dear ~
Tuck my feet in
My old mother would have a fit if she knew ~
Yes, but ~
Drying plates in an earth tray!
Catch me eating off a plate covered in sand!
You'd be the first to complain
Dear ~
Bit of grit in your winkles and you're spitting and spluttering all over the place
Tomorrow, you can just put that thing outside for someone's cat ~ where it belongs!

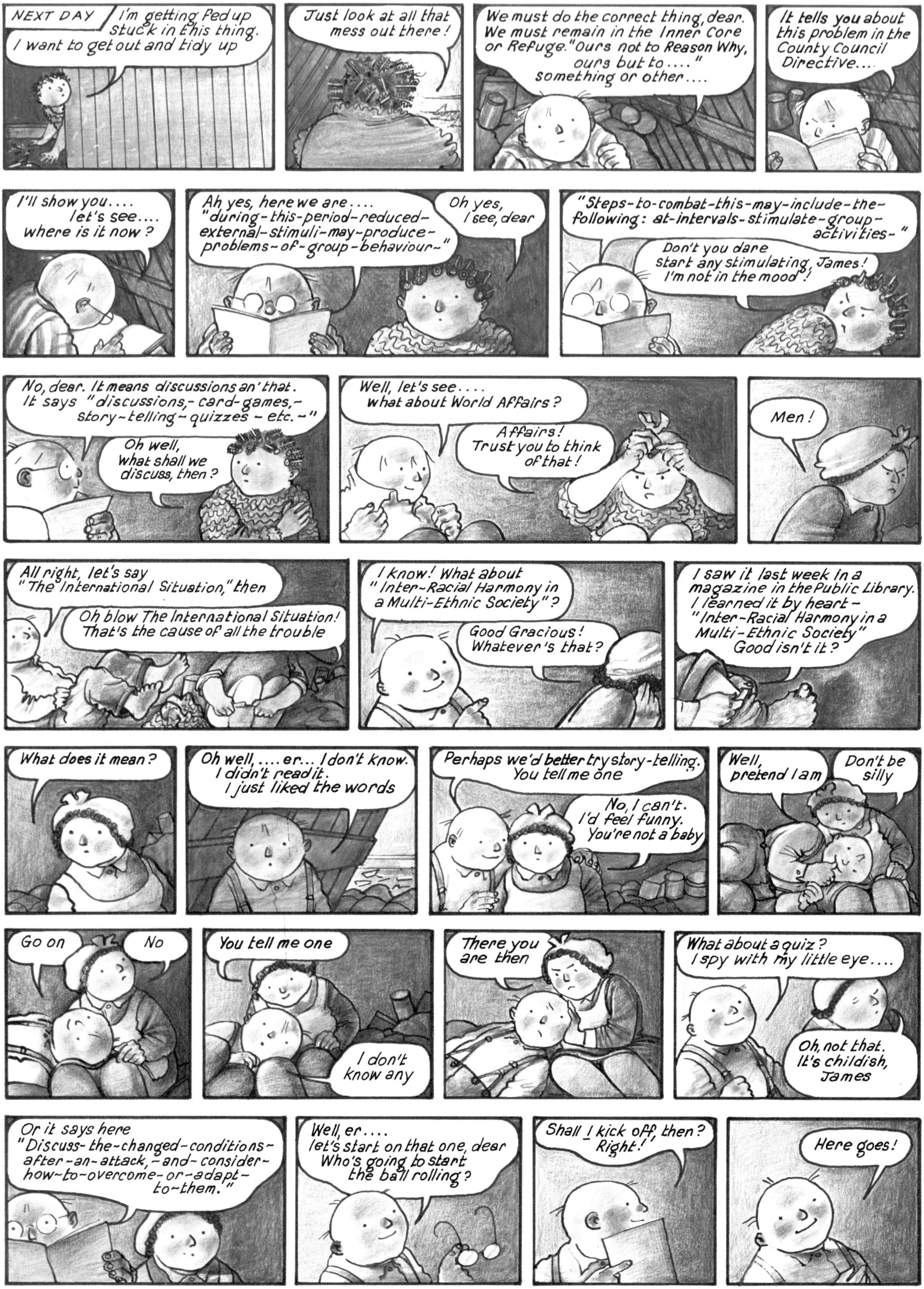
NEXT DAY
I'm getting fed up stuck in this thing. I want to get out and tidy up
Just look at all that mess out there!
We must do the correct thing, dear. We must remain in the Inner Core or Refuge. "Ours not to Reason Why, ours but to...." something or other....
It tells you about this problem in the County Council Directive...
I'll show you.... let's see.... where is it now?
Ah yes, here we are.... "during-this-period-reduced-external-stimuli-may-produce-problems-of-group-behaviour-"
Oh yes, I see, dear
"Steps-to-combat-this-may-include-the-following: at-intervals-stimulate-group-activities-"
Don't you dare start any stimulating, James! I'm not in the mood!
No, dear. It means discussions an' that. It says "discussions,-card-games,-story-telling-quizzes-etc.-"
Oh well, what shall we discuss, then?
Well, let's see.... what about World Affairs?
Affairs! Trust you to think of that!
Men!
All right, let's say "The International Situation," then
Oh blow The International Situation! That's the cause of all the trouble
I know! What about "Inter-Racial Harmony in a Multi-Ethnic Society"?
Good Gracious! Whatever's that?
I saw it last week in a magazine in the Public Library. I learned it by heart - "Inter-Racial Harmony in a Multi-Ethnic Society" Good isn't it?
What does it mean?
Oh well, ... er... I don't know. I didn't read it. I just liked the words
Perhaps we'd better try story-telling. You tell me one
No, I can't. I'd feel funny. You're not a baby
Well, pretend I am
Don't be silly
Go on
No
You tell me one
I don't know any
There you are then
What about a quiz? I spy with my little eye....
Oh, not that. It's childish, James
Or it says here "Discuss-the-changed-conditions-after-an-attack,-and-consider-how-to-overcome-or-adapt-to-them."
Well, er.... let's start on that one, dear Who's going to start the ball rolling?
Shall I kick off, then? Right!
Here goes!

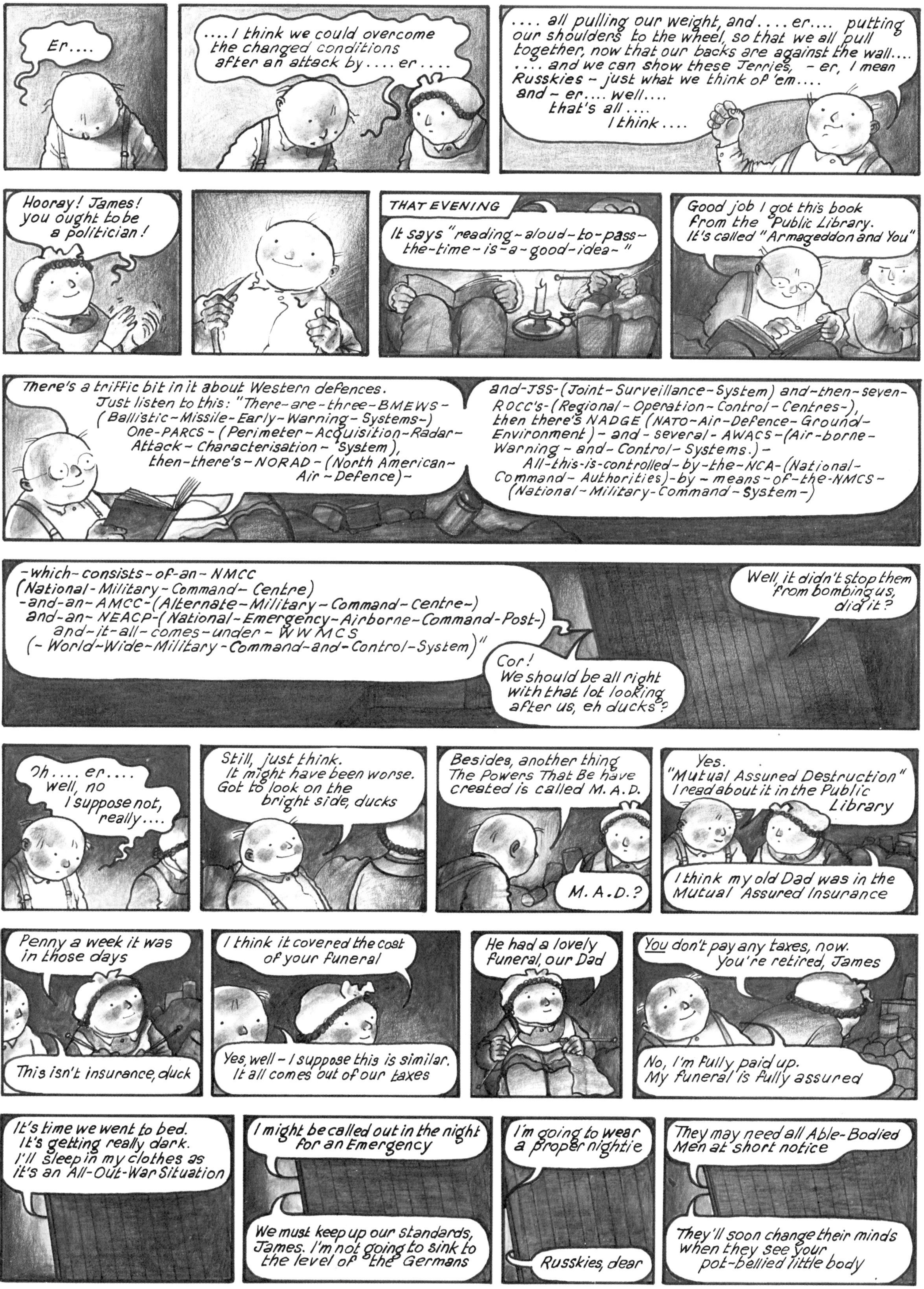
Er....
....I think we could overcome the changed conditions after an attack by....er....
.... all pulling our weight, and....er.... putting our shoulders to the wheel, so that we all pull together, now that our backs are against the wall.... .... and we can show these Jerries, - er, I mean Russkies - just what we think of 'em.... and - er.... well.... that's all.... I think....
Hooray! James! you ought to be a politician!
THAT EVENING
It says "reading-aloud-to-pass-the-time-is-a-good-idea-"
Good job I got this book from the "Public Library. It's called "Armageddon and You"
There's a triffic bit in it about Western defences. Just listen to this: "There-are-three-BMEWS-(Ballistic-Missile-Early-Warning-Systems-) One-PARCS-(Perimeter-Acquisition-Radar-Attack-Characterisation-System), then-there's-NORAD-(North American-Air-Defence)-
and-JSS-(Joint-Surveillance-System) and-then-seven-ROCC's-(Regional-Operation-Control-Centres-), then there's NADGE (NATO-Air-Defence-Ground-Environment)-and-several-AWACS-(Air-borne-Warning-and-Control-Systems.)- All-this-is-controlled-by-the-NCA-(National-Command-Authorities)-by-means-of-the-NMCS-(National-Military-Command-System-)
-which-consists-of-an-NMCC (National-Military-Command-Centre) -and-an-AMCC-(Alternate-Military-Command-Centre-) and-an-NEACP-(National-Emergency-Airborne-Command-Post-) and-it-all-comes-under-WWMCS (-World-Wide-Military-Command-and-Control-System)"
Cor! We should be all right with that lot looking after us, eh ducks?
Well, it didn't stop them from bombing us, did it?
Oh.... er.... well, no I suppose not, really....
Still, just think. It might have been worse. Got to look on the bright side, ducks
Besides, another thing The Powers That Be have created is called M.A.D.
M.A.D.?
Yes. "Mutual Assured Destruction" I read about it in the Public Library
I think my old Dad was in the Mutual Assured Insurance
Penny a week it was in those days
This isn't insurance, duck
I think it covered the cost of your funeral
Yes, well - I suppose this is similar. It all comes out of our taxes
He had a lovely funeral, our Dad
You don't pay any taxes, now. You're retired, James
No, I'm fully paid up. My funeral is fully assured
It's time we went to bed. It's getting really dark. I'll sleep in my clothes as it's an All-Out-War Situation
I might be called out in the night for an Emergency
We must keep up our standards, James. I'm not going to sink to the level of the Germans
I'm going to wear a proper nightie
Russkies, dear
They may need all Able-Bodied Men at short notice
They'll soon change their minds when they see your pot-bellied little body

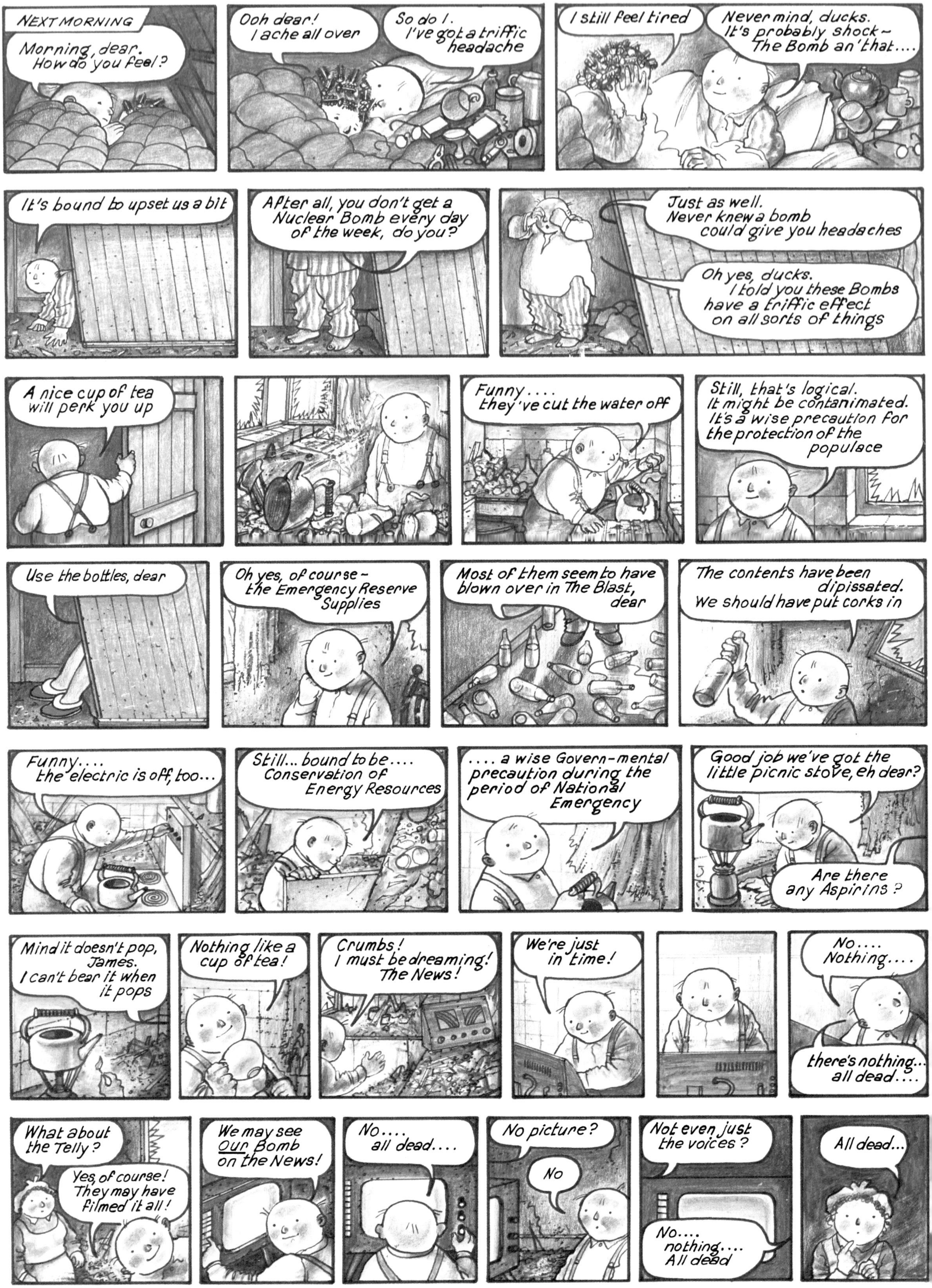
NEXT MORNING
Morning, dear. How do you feel?
Ooh dear! I ache all over
So do I. I've got a triffic headache
I still feel tired
Never mind, ducks. It's probably shock – The Bomb an' that....
It's bound to upset us a bit
After all, you don't get a Nuclear Bomb every day of the week, do you?
Just as well. Never knew a bomb could give you headaches
Oh yes, ducks. I told you these Bombs have a triffic effect on all sorts of things
A nice cup of tea will perk you up
Funny.... they've cut the water off
Still, that's logical. It might be contanimated. It's a wise precaution for the protection of the populace
Use the bottles, dear
Oh yes, of course – the Emergency Reserve Supplies
Most of them seem to have blown over in The Blast, dear
The contents have been dipissated. We should have put corks in
Funny.... the electric is off, too...
Still... bound to be.... Conservation of Energy Resources
.... a wise Govern-mental precaution during the period of National Emergency
Good job we've got the little picnic stove, eh dear?
Are there any Aspirins?
Mind it doesn't pop, James. I can't bear it when it pops
Nothing like a cup of tea!
Crumbs! I must be dreaming! The News!
We're just in time!
No.... Nothing....
there's nothing... all dead....
What about the Telly?
Yes, of course! They may have filmed it all!
We may see Our Bomb on the News!
No.... all dead....
No picture?
No
Not even just the voices?
No.... nothing.... All dead
All dead...

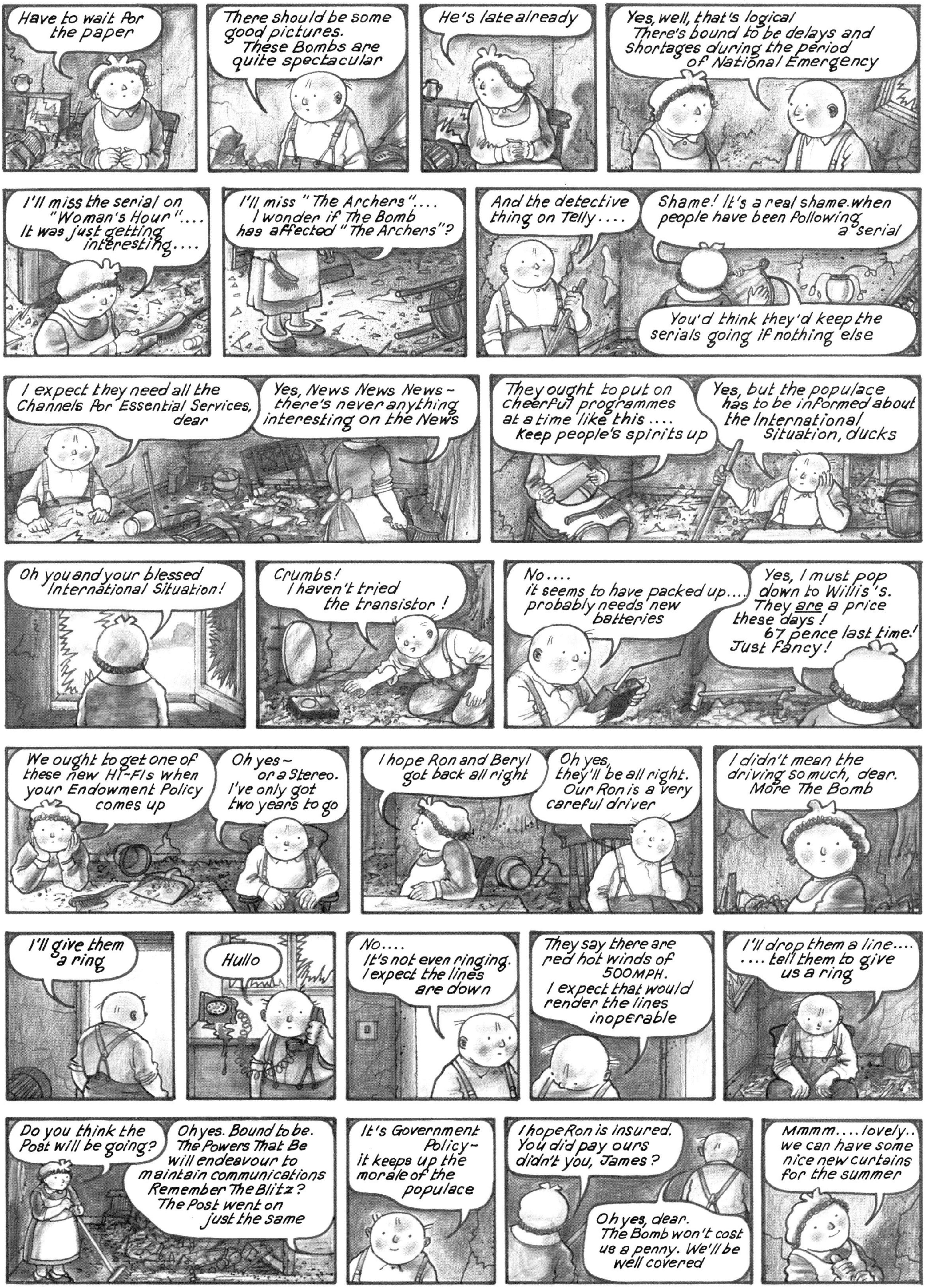
Have to wait for the paper
There should be some good pictures. These Bombs are quite spectacular
He's late already
Yes, well, that's logical There's bound to be delays and shortages during the period of National Emergency
I'll miss the serial on "Woman's Hour".... It was just getting interesting....
I'll miss "The Archers".... I wonder if The Bomb has affected "The Archers"?
And the detective thing on Telly....
Shame! It's a real shame.when people have been following a serial
You'd think they'd keep the serials going if nothing else
I expect they need all the Channels for Essential Services, dear
Yes, News News News - there's never anything interesting on the News
They ought to put on cheerful programmes at a time like this.... Keep people's spirits up
Yes, but the populace has to be informed about the International Situation, ducks
Oh you and your blessed International Situation!
Crumbs! I haven't tried the transistor!
No.... it seems to have packed up.... probably needs new batteries
Yes, I must pop down to Willis's. They are a price these days! 67 pence last time! Just fancy!
We ought to get one of these new HI-FIs when your Endowment Policy comes up
Oh yes - or a Stereo. I've only got two years to go
I hope Ron and Beryl got back all right
Oh yes, they'll be all right. Our Ron is a very careful driver
I didn't mean the driving so much, dear. More The Bomb
I'll give them a ring
Hullo
No.... It's not even ringing. I expect the lines are down
They say there are red hot winds of 500MPH. I expect that would render the lines inoperable
I'll drop them a line.... ....tell them to give us a ring
Do you think the Post will be going?
Oh yes. Bound to be. The Powers That Be will endeavour to maintain communications Remember The Blitz? The Post went on just the same
It's Government Policy - it keeps up the morale of the populace
I hope Ron is insured. You did pay ours didn't you, James?
Oh yes, dear. The Bomb won't cost us a penny. We'll be well covered
Mmmm....lovely.. we can have some nice new curtains for the summer

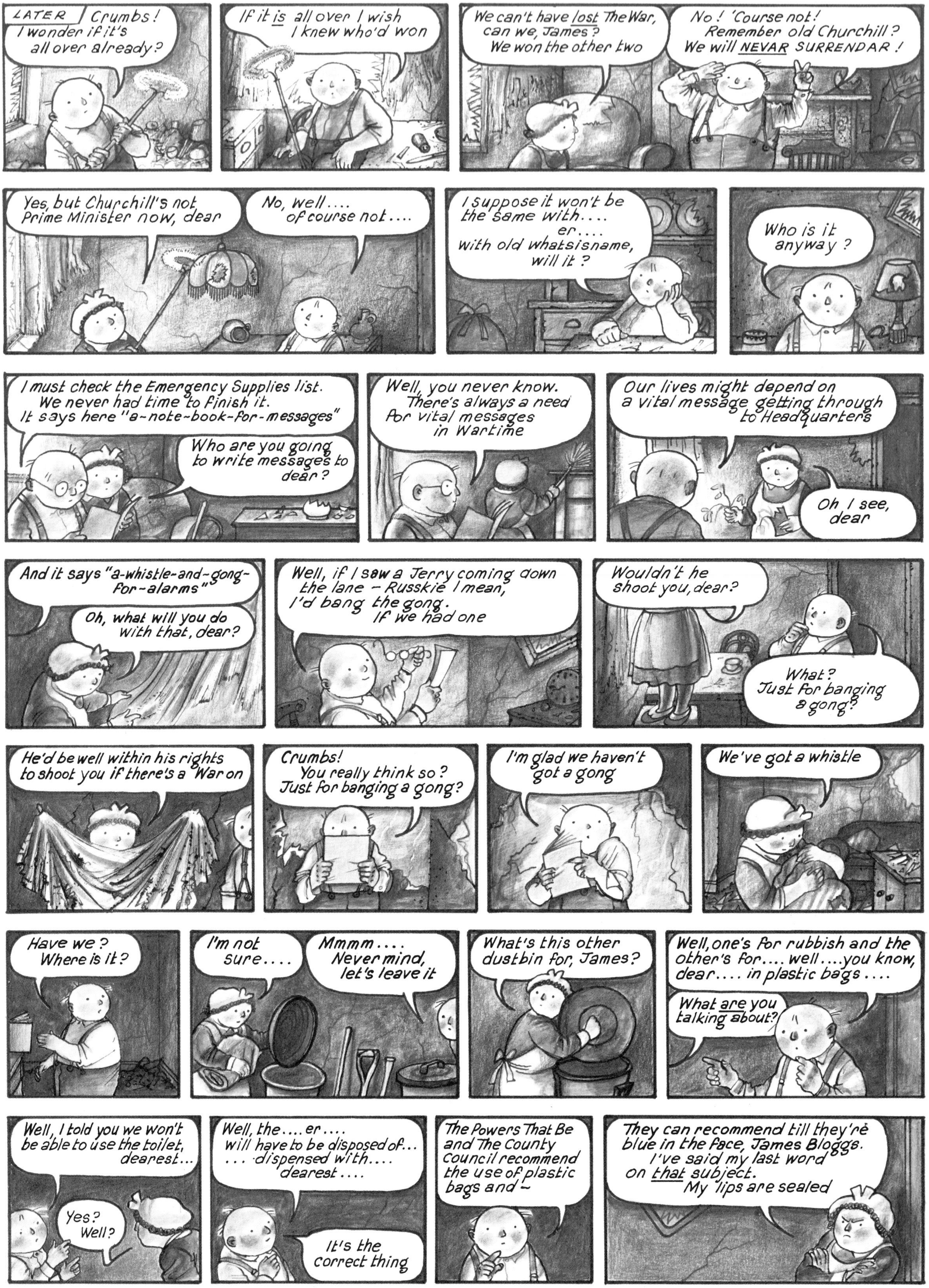
LATER
Crumbs! I wonder if it's all over already?
If it is all over I wish I knew who'd won
We can't have lost The War, can we, James? We won the other two
No! 'Course not! Remember old Churchill? We will NEVAR SURRENDAR!
Yes, but Churchill's not Prime Minister now, dear
No, well.... of course not....
I suppose it won't be the same with.... er.... with old whatsisname, will it?
Who is it anyway?
I must check the Emergency Supplies list. We never had time to finish it. It says here "a-note-book-for-messages"
Who are you going to write messages to dear?
Well, you never know. There's always a need for vital messages in Wartime
Our lives might depend on a vital message getting through to Headquarters
Oh I see, dear
And it says "a-whistle-and-gong-for-alarms"
Oh, what will you do with that, dear?
Well, if I saw a Jerry coming down the lane – Russkie I mean, I'd bang the gong. If we had one
Wouldn't he shoot you, dear?
What? Just for banging a gong?
He'd be well within his rights to shoot you if there's a War on
Crumbs! You really think so? Just for banging a gong?
I'm glad we haven't got a gong
We've got a whistle
Have we? Where is it?
I'm not sure....
Mmmm.... Never mind, let's leave it
What's this other dustbin for, James?
Well, one's for rubbish and the other's for.... well.... you know, dear.... in plastic bags....
What are you talking about?
Well, I told you we won't be able to use the toilet, dearest...
Yes? Well?
Well, the.... er.... will have to be disposed of... ... dispensed with.... dearest....
It's the correct thing
The Powers That Be and The County Council recommend the use of plastic bags and ~
They can recommend till they're blue in the face, James Bloggs. I've said my last word on that subject. My lips are sealed

LATER Oooh! I do feel tired! Really exhausted. And all dizzy....

Nervous Exhaustion due to Unaccustomed Life Style, that's what that is

How is your headache, dear?

Just the same, thanks. Aspirins didn't seem to do any good at all

I think I've got a temperature. I feel all hot and shivery

You do look pale, dear. I should have an early night

I must clear up. Suppose someone comes and sees the place in this state. We might have visitors

Yes. The Emergency Services should arrive today. I'm surprised they've not come before

I expect they've got a lot of people to attend to

Oh yes. We're only an Outlying District. They'll be heavily engaged within the Stricken area itself

Will it be like "Meals on Wheels" dear?

Yes, I should think so. There'll be Mobile Canteens and Soup Kitchens, teams of Doctors and Nurses, helicopters flying in blankets and Medical Supplies — it will all move smoothly into action, you bet. They'll all be here in next to no time

The Govern-mental Authorities have been aware of this eventuality for years, so Continency Plans will have been Formalated long ago

We won't have to worry about a thing. The Powers That Be will get to us in the end

I hope they come soon, dear. I'm not feeling very well

I wonder if we'd have been better off in the cellar?

Oh no, dear. Too damp. Think of my rheumatism

Would you like a bite to eat, dearest?

No thanks. I'm right off food

So am I

I must go to the toilet — and I don't want any arguments!

Blessed dust everywhere!

Oooh! Crumbs! I forgot! We're supposed to stay in the Inner Core or Refuge!

Well, it's too late now. We've been out for ages

Oh Blimey! It was the whole point!

I wonder if there's any Radiation about?

Well, I can't see anything

Hurry up, dear, and get back in the Inner Core or Refuge. We'd better have an early night

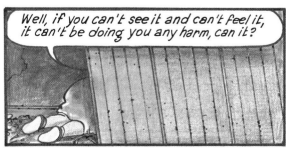

Well, if you can't see it and can't feel it, it can't be doing you any harm, can it?

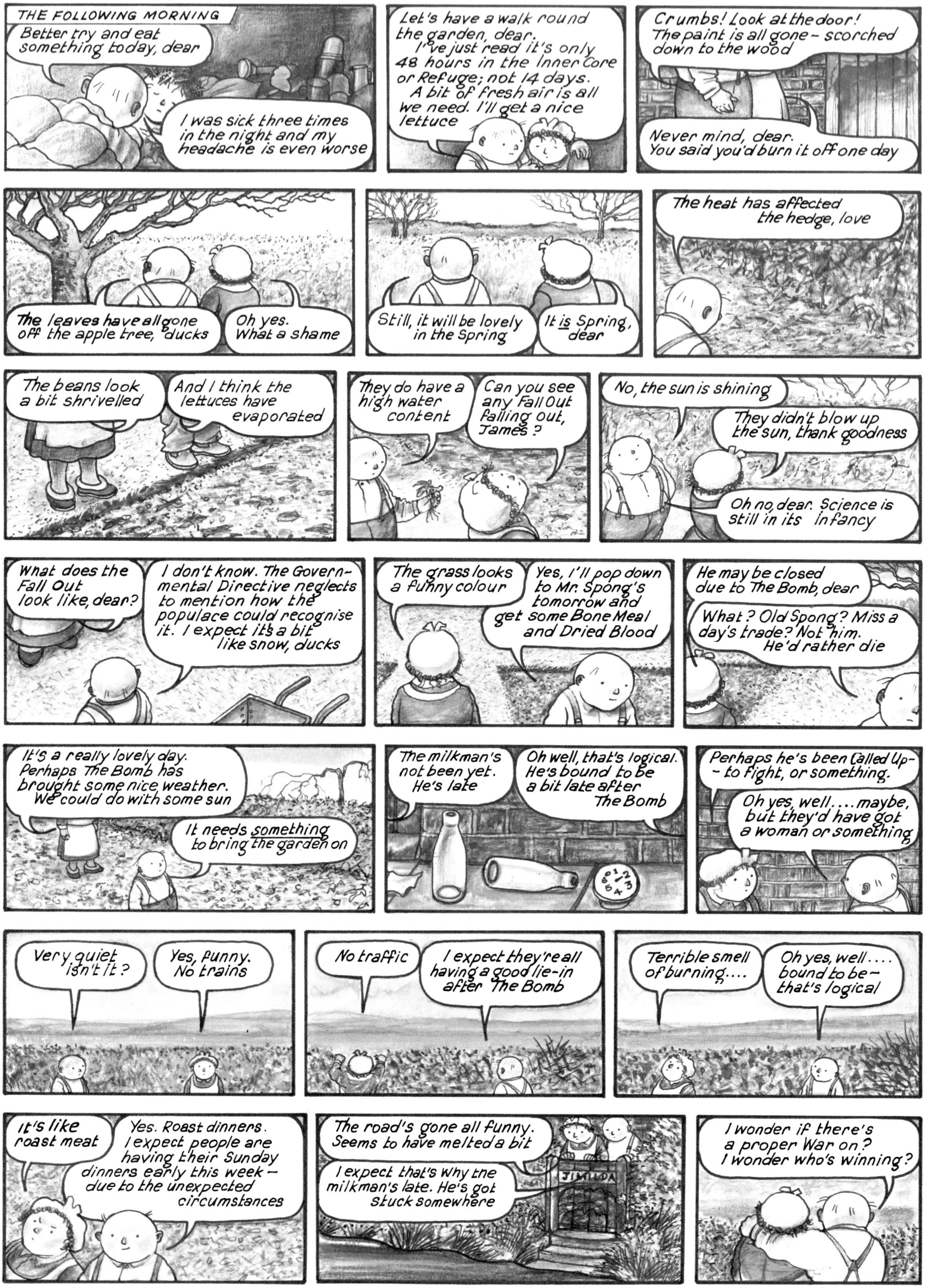
THE FOLLOWING MORNING
Better try and eat something today, dear
I was sick three times in the night and my headache is even worse
Let's have a walk round the garden, dear. I've just read it's only 48 hours in the Inner Core or Refuge; not 14 days. A bit of fresh air is all we need. I'll get a nice lettuce
Crumbs! Look at the door! The paint is all gone – scorched down to the wood
Never mind, dear. You said you'd burn it off one day
The leaves have all gone off the apple tree, ducks
Oh yes. What a shame
Still, it will be lovely in the Spring
It is Spring, dear
The heat has affected the hedge, love
The beans look a bit shrivelled
And I think the lettuces have evaporated
They do have a high water content
Can you see any Fall Out falling out, James?
No, the sun is shining
They didn't blow up the sun, thank goodness
Oh no, dear. Science is still in its infancy
What does the Fall Out look like, dear?
I don't know. The Governmental Directive neglects to mention how the populace could recognise it. I expect it's a bit like snow, ducks
The grass looks a funny colour
Yes, I'll pop down to Mr. Spong's tomorrow and get some Bone Meal and Dried Blood
He may be closed due to The Bomb, dear
What? Old Spong? Miss a day's trade? Not him. He'd rather die
It's a really lovely day. Perhaps The Bomb has brought some nice weather. We could do with some sun
It needs something to bring the garden on
The milkman's not been yet. He's late
Oh well, that's logical. He's bound to be a bit late after The Bomb
Perhaps he's been Called Up – to Fight, or something.
Oh yes, well.... maybe, but they'd have got a woman or something
Very quiet isn't it?
Yes, funny. No trains
No traffic
I expect they're all having a good lie-in after The Bomb
Terrible smell of burning....
Oh yes, well.... bound to be – that's logical
It's like roast meat
Yes. Roast dinners. I expect people are having their Sunday dinners early this week – due to the unexpected circumstances
The road's gone all funny. Seems to have melted a bit
I expect that's why the milkman's late. He's got stuck somewhere
JIMHILDA
I wonder if there's a proper War on? I wonder who's winning?

Never mind. It'll all be in the papers, dear

Come to think of it – he's late, too

He missed us altogether yesterday

Well, you can't expect things to be normal after The Bomb. Difficulties will be experienced throughout the Duration of the Emergency Period

Normality will only be assumed after the Censation of Hostilities

Oh dear – I think I'm going to be sick again

There, there, ducks, all better now

I had the most terrible diarrhoea this morning

Nerves, dear. Just nerves. I'm the same and I'm a man

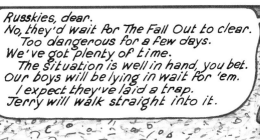
Let's sit in the sun for a bit

Don't you think we ought to clear up, dear?

Yes, later on. I feel a bit weak and dizzy. We'll make a start soon

Oooh! Suppose Jerry comes this afternoon!

Russkies, dear.
No, they'd wait for The Fall Out to clear.
Too dangerous for a few days.
We've got plenty of time.
The situation is well in hand, you bet.
Our boys will be lying in wait for 'em.
I expect they've laid a trap.
Jerry will walk straight into it.

Hullo.... sun's gone in. Cloud coming up. Looks like rain....

LATER
It's raining. I'm going in

RAIN! Yes! We can save it!

Don't you get wet, James! You'll catch your death

We'll be all right for water for a while now, dear

Do you think rain water is all right to drink?

Oh yes! 'Course it is! There's nothing purer than rainwater is there? Everybody knows that

Perhaps I'd better boil it. Best to be on the safe side

Oh yes, I suppose so. We don't want to take any unnecessary risks

It may prejudice our chance of survival

What do you mean, James? We have survived, haven't we?

Yes, I know, but after The Bombs on Japan, people died ages later .... I forget exactly why ....

Perhaps they didn't take precautions

Yes. I expect they neglected to do the correct thing.
And anyway, that was years ago. Science was in its infancy.
We're better equipped to deal with the situation in the light of modern scientific knowledge

Yes, nowadays there's bound to be all sorts of andi-totes and protectives

When the Medics get through, they'll probably just spray us with some andi-tote, give us a couple of pills and in no time we'll be as right as rain

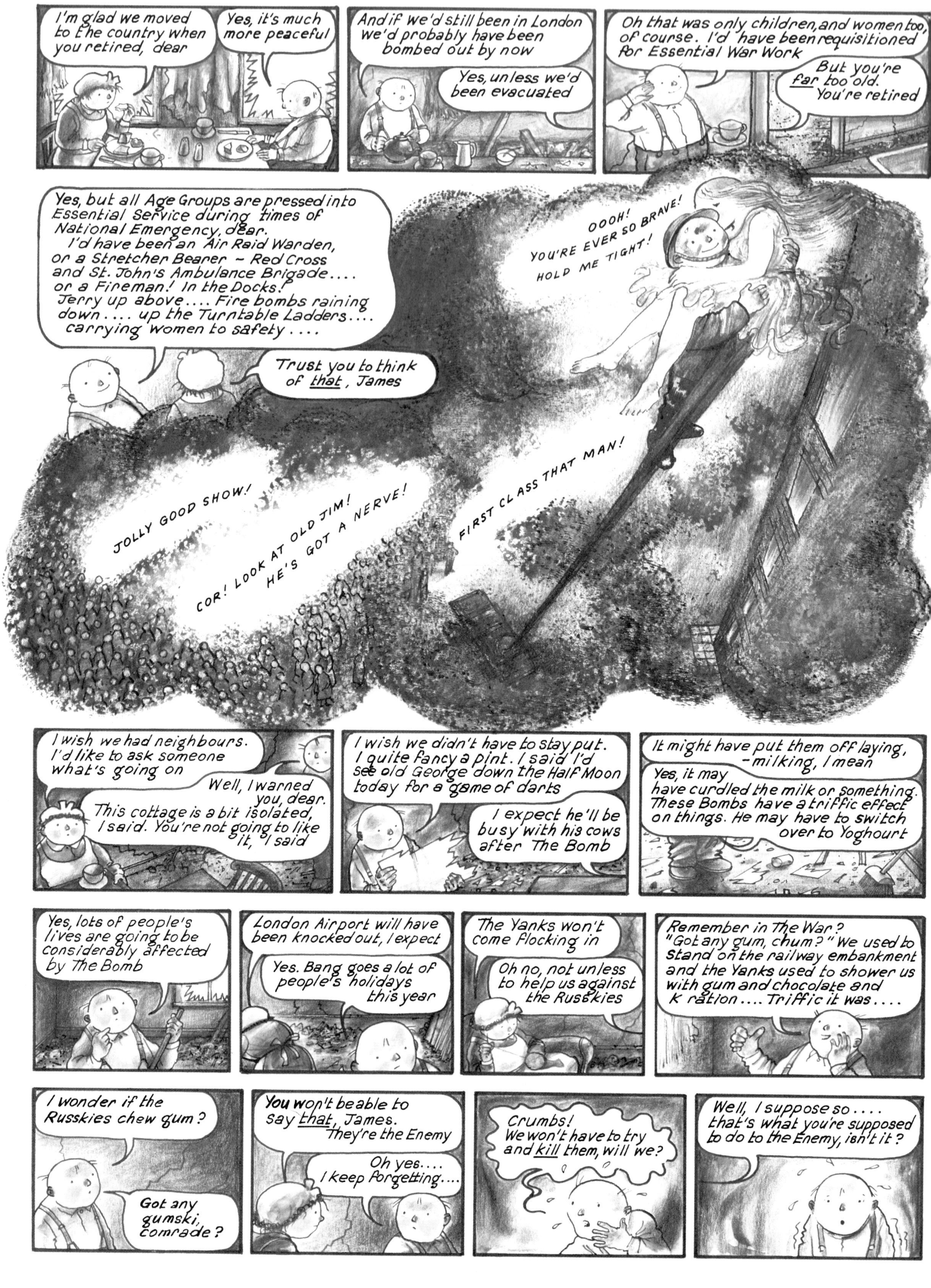

I'm glad we moved to the country when you retired, dear
Yes, it's much more peaceful
And if we'd still been in London we'd probably have been bombed out by now
Yes, unless we'd been evacuated
Oh that was only children, and women too, of course. I'd have been requisitioned for Essential War Work
But you're far too old. You're retired
Yes, but all Age Groups are pressed into Essential Service during times of National Emergency, dear. I'd have been an Air Raid Warden, or a Stretcher Bearer ~ Red Cross and St. John's Ambulance Brigade.... or a Fireman! In the Docks! Jerry up above.... Fire bombs raining down.... up the Turntable Ladders.... carrying women to safety....
Trust you to think of that, James
OOOH! YOU'RE EVER SO BRAVE! HOLD ME TIGHT!
JOLLY GOOD SHOW!
COR! LOOK AT OLD JIM! HE'S GOT A NERVE!
FIRST CLASS THAT MAN!
I wish we had neighbours. I'd like to ask someone what's going on
Well, I warned you, dear. This cottage is a bit isolated, I said. You're not going to like it, I said
I wish we didn't have to stay put. I quite fancy a pint. I said I'd see old George down the Half Moon today for a game of darts
I expect he'll be busy with his cows after The Bomb
It might have put them off laying, - milking, I mean
Yes, it may have curdled the milk or something. These Bombs have a triffic effect on things. He may have to switch over to Yoghourt
Yes, lots of people's lives are going to be considerably affected by The Bomb
London Airport will have been knocked out, I expect
Yes. Bang goes a lot of people's holidays this year
The Yanks won't come flocking in
Oh no, not unless to help us against the Russkies
Remember in The War? "Got any gum, chum?" We used to stand on the railway embankment and the Yanks used to shower us with gum and chocolate and K ration.... Triffic it was....
I wonder if the Russkies chew gum?
Got any gumski, comrade?
You won't be able to say that, James. They're the Enemy
Oh yes.... I keep forgetting....
Crumbs! We won't have to try and kill them, will we?
Well, I suppose so.... that's what you're supposed to do to the Enemy, isn't it?

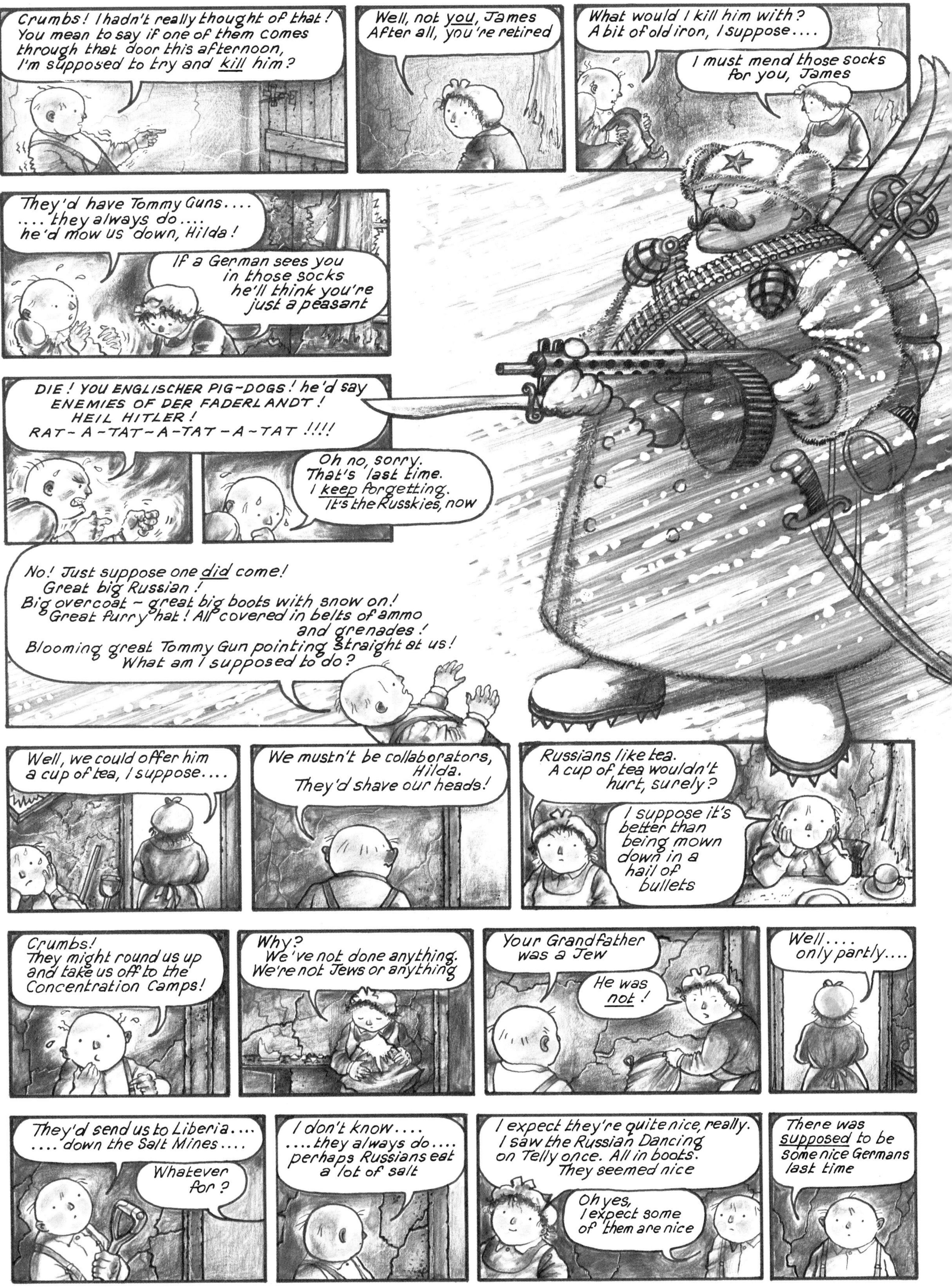

Crumbs! I hadn't really thought of that! You mean to say if one of them comes through that door this afternoon, I'm supposed to try and kill him?
Well, not you, James After all, you're retired
What would I kill him with? A bit of old iron, I suppose....
I must mend those socks for you, James
They'd have Tommy Guns.... ....they always do.... he'd mow us down, Hilda!
If a German sees you in those socks he'll think you're just a peasant
DIE! YOU ENGLISCHER PIG-DOGS! he'd say ENEMIES OF DER FADERLANDT! HEIL HITLER! RAT-A-TAT-A-TAT-A-TAT!!!!
Oh no, sorry. That's last time. I keep forgetting. It's the Russkies, now
No! Just suppose one did come! Great big Russian! Big overcoat - great big boots with snow on! Great furry hat! All covered in belts of ammo and grenades! Blooming great Tommy Gun pointing straight at us! What am I supposed to do?
Well, we could offer him a cup of tea, I suppose....
We mustn't be collaborators, Hilda. They'd shave our heads!
Russians like tea. A cup of tea wouldn't hurt, surely?
I suppose it's better than being mown down in a hail of bullets
Crumbs! They might round us up and take us off to the Concentration Camps!
Why? We've not done anything. We're not Jews or anything
Your Grandfather was a Jew
He was not!
Well.... only partly....
They'd send us to Liberia.... ....down the Salt Mines....
Whatever for?
I don't know.... ....they always do.... perhaps Russians eat a lot of salt
I expect they're quite nice, really. I saw the Russian Dancing on Telly once. All in boots. They seemed nice
Oh yes, I expect some of them are nice
There was supposed to be some nice Germans last time

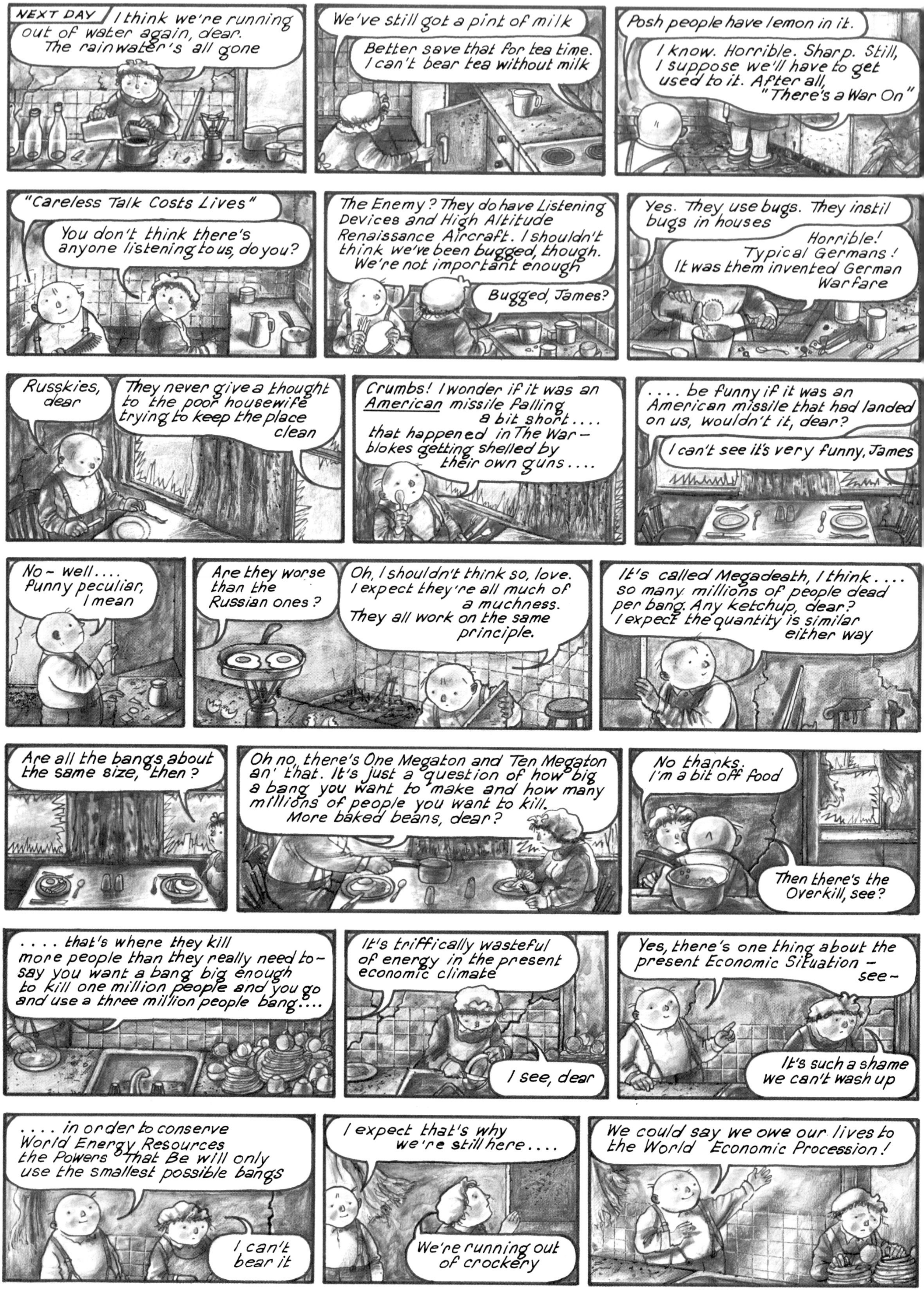
NEXT DAY
I think we're running out of water again, dear. The rainwater's all gone
We've still got a pint of milk
Better save that for tea time. I can't bear tea without milk
Posh people have lemon in it.
I know. Horrible. Sharp. Still, I suppose we'll have to get used to it. After all, "There's a War On"
"Careless Talk Costs Lives"
You don't think there's anyone listening to us, do you?
The Enemy? They do have Listening Devices and High Altitude Renaissance Aircraft. I shouldn't think we've been bugged, though. We're not important enough
Bugged, James?
Yes. They use bugs. They instil bugs in houses
Horrible! Typical Germans! It was them invented German Warfare
Russkies, dear
They never give a thought to the poor housewife trying to keep the place clean
Crumbs! I wonder if it was an American missile falling a bit short.... that happened in The War – blokes getting shelled by their own guns....
.... be funny if it was an American missile that had landed on us, wouldn't it, dear?
I can't see it's very funny, James
No – well.... funny peculiar, I mean
Are they worse than the Russian ones?
Oh, I shouldn't think so, love. I expect they're all much of a muchness. They all work on the same principle.
It's called Megadeath, I think.... so many millions of people dead per bang. Any ketchup, dear? I expect the quantity is similar either way
Are all the bangs about the same size, then?
Oh no, there's One Megaton and Ten Megaton an' that. It's just a question of how big a bang you want to make and how many millions of people you want to kill. More baked beans, dear?
No thanks. I'm a bit off food
Then there's the Overkill, see?
.... that's where they kill more people than they really need to – say you want a bang big enough to kill one million people and you go and use a three million people bang....
It's triffically wasteful of energy in the present economic climate
I see, dear
Yes, there's one thing about the present Economic Situation – see –
It's such a shame we can't wash up
.... in order to conserve World Energy Resources the Powers That Be will only use the smallest possible bangs
I can't bear it
I expect that's why we're still here....
We're running out of crockery
We could say we owe our lives to the World Economic Procession!

Put the kettle on will you, ducks?

There's no water, dear

Oh no, of course. Just have to have milk, then

That pint has gone bad, dear. The fridge has been off....

Oh heck! Well .... black coffee, then

There's still no water, dear

Well, what are we going to drink?

Eh? EH?

WHAT ARE WE GOING TO DRINK FOR GOD'S SAKE?

Don't shout, dearest

I'm sorry, love – I'm just terribly thirsty

How about a nice sweet, dear?

There's only one left. It's a Blackcurrant Throat Pastille

You have it

No. You have it

We'll cut it in half, that's fair

LATER

EEEEEEEEEEK!

I'm coming! I'm coming!

There's a RAT!! A RAT!! A rat in the lavatory!

Oooh! Oooh! I saw it! Its tail was waving in the pan!

Never mind, it won't hurt you, dearest

– the pan's all dry and.... ... and its head was round the bend just its bottom end sticking out.... the tail.... Oooh! The tail....

Horrible! Horrible!

There There

I'll pop down to Willis's in the morning– get some Warfaring

At least it shows the drains aren't blocked

Oh dear, I do feel queer.... all shaky....

Well, it's bound to upset you a bit, The Bomb, I mean

We'll just have to acclimatise ourselves to the Post-Nuclear Area. It could be OK – wiping the slate clean.... starting afresh – A New World! Perjured of all the Old Vices – like London after The Fire of London! The New Elizabethan Age will dawn! Britannia will rise again with fresh fields and pastures new to conquer! The Old Empire will live again – rising like a phenis from the ashes!

Have you got lipstick on dear?

Lipstick? What do you mean, James

You know I haven't worn lipstick for years

Well, your lips are all red

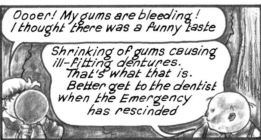
Oooer! My gums are bleeding! I thought there was a funny taste

Shrinking of gums causing ill-fitting dentures. That's what that is. Better get to the dentist when the Emergency has rescinded

There was blood when I went to the toilet this morning

Yes, me too. Piles that is, Hovaloyds. A common complaint in middle-aged people like ourselves

I'll pop down the Chemist's when the crisis pales into insignifiance – get some of those suppostories

Oh dear, I think I'm going to be sick....

There, there, ducks. All better now....

Don't upset yourself, love. Don't cry. I expect it's due to the Vibration

Like being in a car.... you remember that time we went to Bournemouth and you were sick in the coach?

Don't worry, ducks. There can't be anything wrong with you. I expect it's just the after-effects of The Bomb

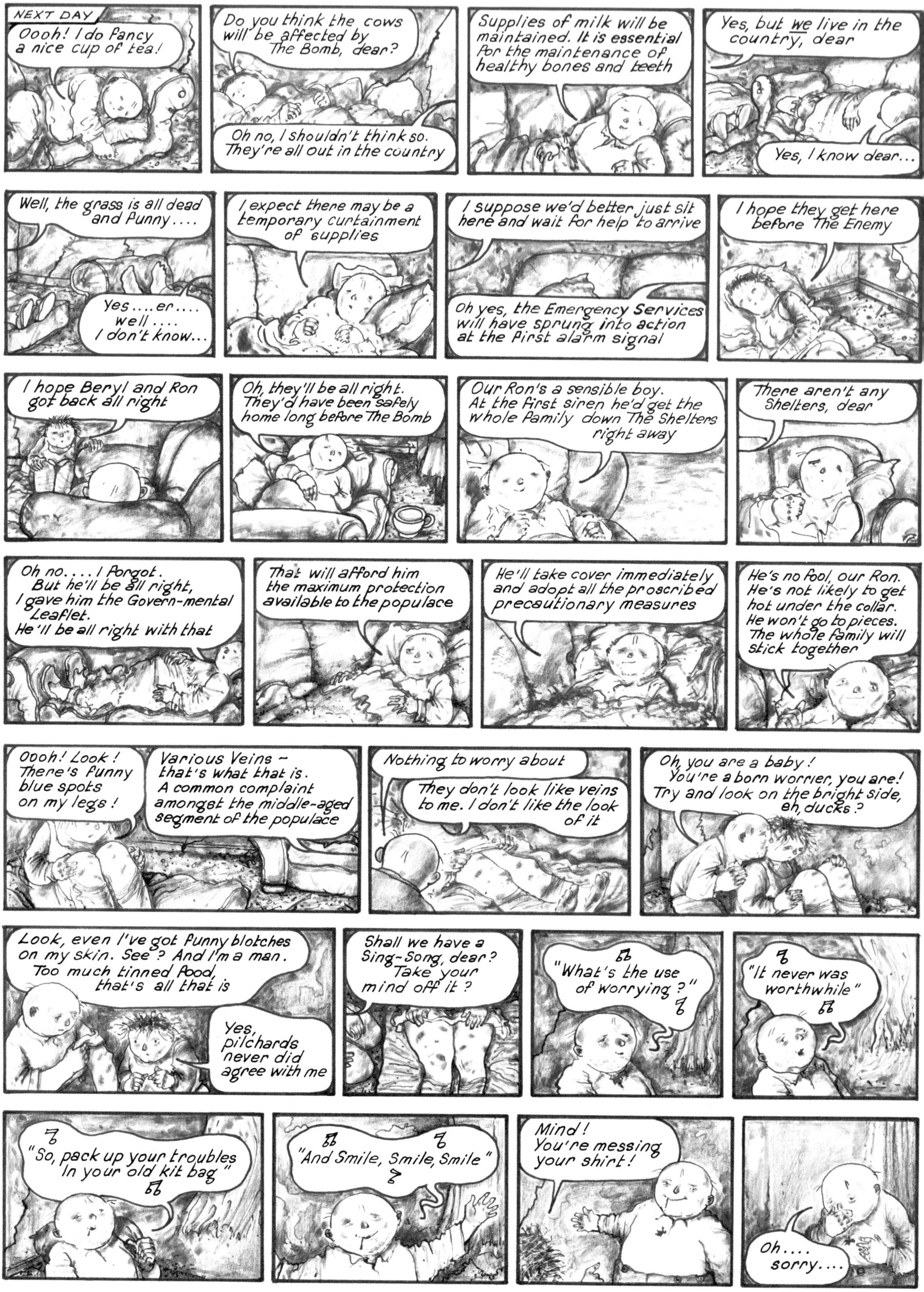
NEXT DAY
Oooh! I do fancy a nice cup of tea!
Do you think the cows will be affected by The Bomb, dear?
Oh no, I shouldn't think so. They're all out in the country
Supplies of milk will be maintained. It is essential for the maintenance of healthy bones and teeth
Yes, but we live in the country, dear
Yes, I know dear...
Well, the grass is all dead and funny....
Yes....er.... well.... I don't know...
I expect there may be a temporary curtainment of supplies
I suppose we'd better just sit here and wait for help to arrive
Oh yes, the Emergency Services will have sprung into action at the first alarm signal
I hope they get here before The Enemy
I hope Beryl and Ron got back all right
Oh, they'll be all right. They'd have been safely home long before The Bomb
Our Ron's a sensible boy. At the first siren he'd get the whole family down The Shelters right away
There aren't any Shelters, dear
Oh no.... I forgot. But he'll be all right, I gave him the Govern-mental Leaflet. He'll be all right with that
That will afford him the maximum protection available to the populace
He'll take cover immediately and adopt all the proscribed precautionary measures
He's no fool, our Ron. He's not likely to get hot under the collar. He won't go to pieces. The whole family will stick together
Oooh! Look! There's funny blue spots on my legs!
Various Veins – that's what that is. A common complaint amongst the middle-aged segment of the populace
Nothing to worry about
They don't look like veins to me. I don't like the look of it
Oh, you are a baby! You're a born worrier, you are! Try and look on the bright side, eh, ducks?
Look, even I've got funny blotches on my skin. See? And I'm a man. Too much tinned food, that's all that is
Yes, pilchards never did agree with me
Shall we have a Sing-Song, dear? Take your mind off it?
"What's the use of worrying?"
"It never was worthwhile"
"So, pack up your troubles In your old kit bag"
"And Smile, Smile, Smile"
Mind! You're messing your shirt!
Oh.... sorry....

Must put some Germolene on these spots

Yes, they'll soon clear up

I'll pop down the Chemist's in the morning. Get some Savlon

Yes. We could do with some Lozenges or Pastilles, too. I've still got a terrible throat

So have I. I wonder if he'll be able to sell us some water?

I'm going to have an early night, James

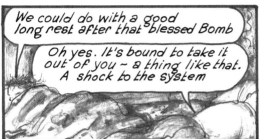
We could do with a good long rest after that blessed Bomb

Oh yes. It's bound to take it out of you ~ a thing like that. A shock to the system

Oh yes. It's bound to shake you up a bit

I expect it affects the aeons in the atmosphere

Yes. I expect so

Oooh! Look! My hair's coming out!

Don't worry, dearest. Women don't go bald. That's a scientific fact

Shall we get into those paper bags again?

Whatever For, dear?

Well, you never know. There might be another one while we're asleep

I suppose it wouldn't hurt. It would be a sensible precautionary measure in the circumstances

After all, this is an All Out War Situation

Another I B M might come over....

Oooh! It's stuffy in these bags!

Now you know what it feels like to be a potato!

Yes. I should hate that - being buried in the ground

Oh, so would I. Give me cremation every time

Oh, me too

We'd better just lie here and wait for The Emergency Services to arrive

Yes, they'll take good care of us

We won't have to worry about a thing

Just leave everything to them....

.... they'll know what to do

Yes, ... the Govern~mental Authorities will know what to do with us ....

The Powers That Be will get to us in the end....

You have got the box with our Medical Cards and Birth Certificates, haven't you?

Yes, dear They're quite safe

Night, night, Hilda

Night, Night, Jimmy, dear

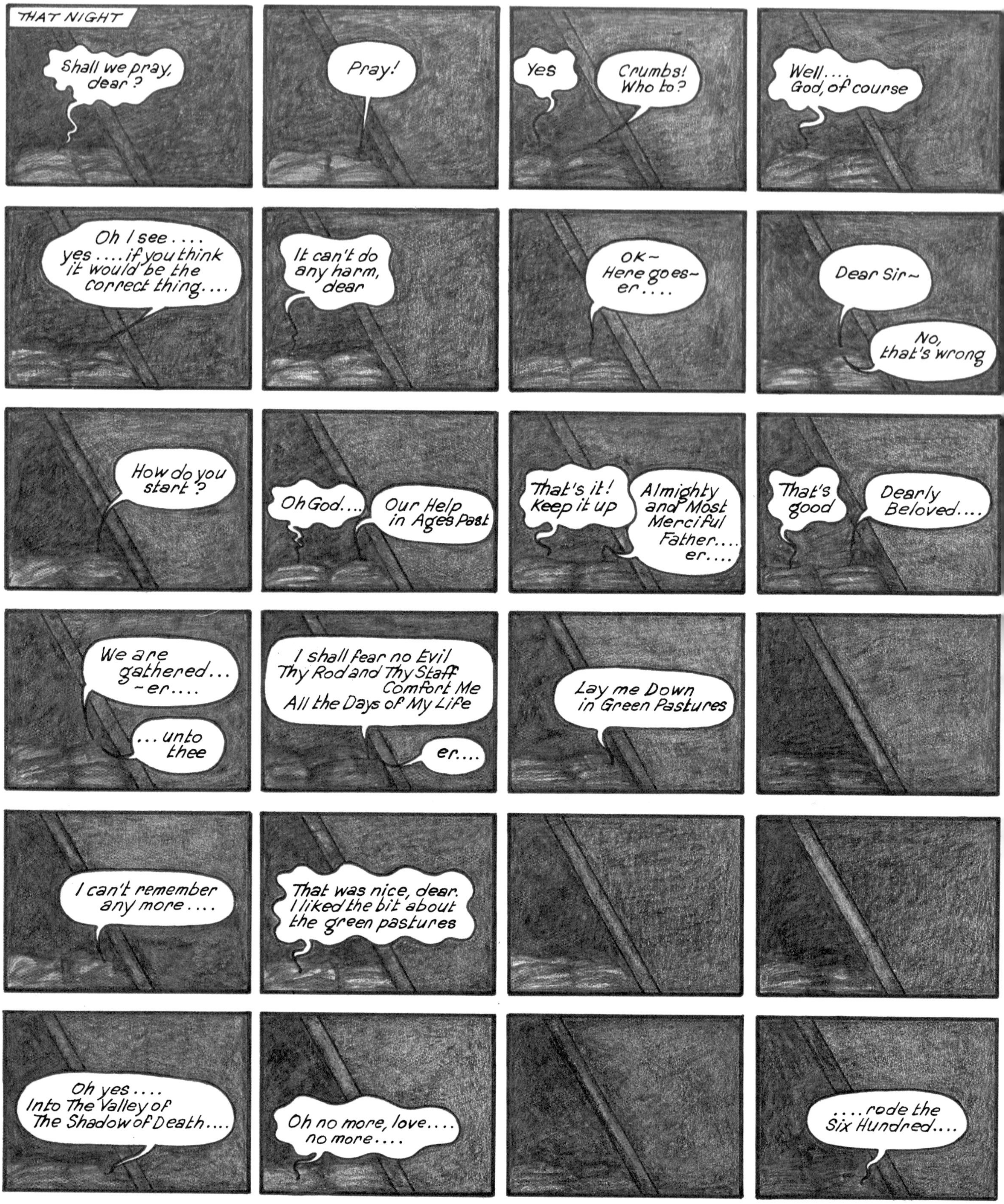
THAT NIGHT
Shall we pray, dear?
Pray!
Yes
Crumbs! Who to?
Well.... God, of course
Oh I see.... yes.... if you think it would be the correct thing....
It can't do any harm, dear
OK~ Here goes~ er....
Dear Sir~
No, that's wrong
How do you start?
Oh God....
Our Help in Ages Past
That's it! Keep it up
Almighty and Most Merciful Father.... er....
That's good
Dearly Beloved....
We are gathered... ~er....
...unto thee
I shall fear no Evil Thy Rod and Thy Staff Comfort Me All the Days of My Life
er....
Lay me Down in Green Pastures
I can't remember any more....
That was nice, dear. I liked the bit about the green pastures
Oh yes.... Into The Valley of The Shadow of Death....
Oh no more, love.... no more....
....rode the Six Hundred....